P9-AFJ-547

Another Marvelous Thing

Another
Marvelous
Thing

LAURIE COLWIN

Alfred A. Knopf New York 1986

THIS IS A BORZOI BOOK
PUBLISHED BY ALFRED A. KNOPF, INC.

Copyright © 1982, 1983, 1984, 1985, 1986 by Laurie Colwin
All rights reserved under International and
Pan-American Copyright Conventions. Published in
the United States by Alfred A. Knopf, Inc., New York,
and simultaneously in Canada by Random House of
Canada Limited, Toronto. Distributed by Random
House, Inc., New York.

"Frank and Billy" and "French Movie" originally appeared
in *Cosmopolitan*. "A Little Something" originally appeared
in *New Woman*. "Another Marvelous Thing," "A Country Wedding,"
"A Couple of Old Flames" (originally entitled "Old Flames"),
and "Swan Song" originally appeared in *The New Yorker*.
"My Mistress" originally appeared in *Playboy*.
Grateful acknowledgment is made to Farrar, Straus & Giroux, Inc.
for permission to reprint an excerpt from "Falling in Love Is
Never as Simple" by Randall Jarrell from *The Complete Poems*
by Randall Jarrell. Copyright 1937, renewed © 1969 by Mrs.
Randall Jarrell. Reprinted by permission of
Farrar, Straus & Giroux, Inc.

Library of Congress Cataloging-in-Publication Data
Colwin, Laurie.
Another marvelous thing.
I. Title.
PS3553.04783A8   1985   813'.54   85-45588
ISBN 0-394-55128-1

Manufactured in the United States of America
FIRST EDITION

Laurie Colwin wishes to thank
the National Endowment for the Arts
for its generous support.

For
Candida Donadio
and to
Audrey Jacobson, Linda Faulhaber,
and Alice Quinn

Falling in love is never as simple
As love and the lady novelists say;
Love's least sneeze may take, may rankle,
The thousand nights be as bad as day.
Instead of responding like an apple,
You fall in your own unfortunate way.

—Randall Jarrell

Contents

Another Marvelous Thing

My Mistress

My wife is precise, elegant, and well-dressed, but the sloppiness of my mistress knows few bounds. Apparently I am not the sort of man who acquires a stylish mistress—the mistresses in French movies who rendezvous at the cafés in expensive hotels and take their cigarette cases out of alligator handbags, or meet their lovers on bridges wearing dashing capes. My mistress greets me in a pair of worn corduroy trousers, once green and now no color at all, a gray sweater, an old shirt of her younger brother's which has a frayed collar, and a pair of very old, broken shoes with tassels, the backs of which are held together with electrical tape. The first time I saw these shoes I found them remarkable.

"What are those?" I said. "Why do you wear them?"

My mistress is a serious, often glum person, who likes to put as little inflection into a sentence as she can.

"They used to be quite nice," she said. "I wore them out. Now I use them for slippers. They are my house shoes."

This person's name is Josephine Delielle, nicknamed Billy. I am Francis Clemens, and no one but my mistress calls me

Frank. The first time we went to bed, my mistress fixed me with an indifferent stare and said: "Isn't this nice. In bed with Frank and Billy."

My constant image of Billy is of her pushing her hair off her forehead with an expression of exasperation on her face. She frowns easily, often looks puzzled, and is frequently irritated. In movies men have mistresses who soothe and pet them, who are consoling, passionate, and ornamental. But I have a mistress who is mostly grumpy. Traditional things mean nothing to her. She does not flirt, cajole, or wear fancy underwear. She has taken to referring to me as her "little bit of fluff," or she calls me *her* mistress, as in the sentence: "Before you became my mistress I led a blameless life."

But in spite of this I am secure in her affections. I know she loves me—not that she would ever come right out and tell me. She prefers the oblique line of approach. She may say something like: "Being in love with you is making me a nervous wreck."

Here is a typical encounter. It is between two and three o'clock in the afternoon. I arrive and ring the doorbell. The Delielles, who seem to have a lot of money, live in a duplex apartment in an old town house. Billy opens the door. There I am, an older man in my tweed coat. My hands are cold. I'd like to get them underneath her ratty sweater. She looks me up and down. She gives me her edition of a smile—a repressed smile that is half smirk, half grin.

Sometimes she gets her coat and we go for a bracing walk. Sometimes we go upstairs to her study. Billy is an economic historian who teaches two classes at the business school. She writes for a couple of highbrow journals. Her husband, Grey, is the resident economics genius at a think tank. They are one of those dashing couples, or at least they sound like one. I am no slouch either. For years I was an investment banker, and now I consult from my own home. I too write for a couple of highbrow journals. We have much in common, my mistress and I, or so it looks.

Billy's study is untidy. She likes to spread her papers out. Since her surroundings mean nothing to her, her work place is bare of ornament, a cheerless, dreary little space.

"What have you been doing all day?" she says.

I tell her. Breakfast with my wife, Vera; newspaper reading after Vera has gone to work; an hour or so on the telephone with clients; a walk to my local bookstore; more telephoning; a quick sandwich; her.

"You and I ought to go out to lunch some day," she says. "One should always take one's mistress out for lunch. We could go dutch, thereby taking both mistresses at once."

"I try to take you for lunch," I say. "But you don't like to be taken out for lunch."

"Huh," utters Billy. She stares at her bookcase as if looking for a misplaced volume and then she may give me a look that might translate into something tender such as: "If I gave you a couple of dollars, would you take your clothes off?"

Instead, I take her into my arms. Her words are my signal that Grey is out of town. Often he is not, and then I merely get to kiss my mistress which makes us both dizzy. To kiss her and know that we can go forward to what Billy tonelessly refers to as "the rapturous consummation" reminds me that in relief is joy.

After kissing for a few minutes, Billy closes the study door and we practically throw ourselves at one another. After the rapturous consummation has been achieved, during which I can look upon a mistress recognizable as such to me, my mistress will turn to me and in a voice full of the attempt to stifle emotion say something like: "Sometimes I don't understand how I got so fond of a beat-up old person such as you."

These are the joys adulterous love brings to me.

Billy is indifferent to a great many things: clothes, food, home decor. She wears neither perfume nor cologne. She uses what is used on infants: baby powder and Ivory soap. She hates to cook and will never present me with an interesting postcoital snack. Her snacking habits are those, I have often remarked, of a dyspeptic nineteenth-century English clubman. Billy will get up and present me with a mug of cold tea, a plate of hard wheat biscuits, or a squirt of tepid soda from the siphon on her desk. As she sits under her quilt nibbling those resistant biscuits, she reminds me of a creature from another universe—the solar system that contains the alien features of her real life: her past, her marriage, why I am in her life, what she thinks of me.

I drink my soda, put on my clothes, and, unless Vera is out of town, I go home to dinner. If Vera and Grey are out of town at the same time, which happens every now and again, Billy and I go out to dinner, during the course of which she either falls asleep or looks as if she is about to. Then I take her home, go home myself, and have a large steadying drink.

I was not entirely a stranger to adulterous love when I met Billy. I have explained this to her. In all long marriages, I expound, there are certain lapses. The look on Billy's face as I lecture is one of either amusement or contempt or both. The dinner party you are invited to as an extra man when your wife is away, I tell her. You are asked to take the extra woman, whose husband is also away, home in a taxi. The divorced family friend who invites you in for a drink one night, and so on. These fallings into bed are the friendliest thing in the world, I add. I look at my mistress.

"I see," she says. "Just like patting a dog."

My affair with Billy, as she well knows, is nothing of the sort. I call her every morning. I see her almost every weekday afternoon. On the days she teaches, she calls me. We are as faithful as the Canada goose, more or less. She is an absolute fact of my life. When not at work, and when not with her, my thoughts rest upon the subject of her as easily as you might lay a hand on a child's head. I conduct a mental life with her when we are apart. Thinking about her is like entering a secret room to which only I have access.

I, too, am part of a dashing couple. My wife is an interior designer who has dozens of commissions and consults to practically everyone. Our two sons are grown up. One is a securities analyst and one is a journalist. What a lively table we must be, all of us together. So I tell my mistress. She gives me a baleful look.

"We can get plenty of swell types in for meals," she says.

I know this is true and I know that Billy, unlike my gregarious and party-giving wife, thinks that there is no hell more hellish than the hell of social life. She has made up a tuneless little chant, like a football cheer, to describe it. It goes:

> *They invited us*
> *We invited them*
> *They invited us*
> *We invited them*
> *They invited us*
> *We invited them*

Billy and I met at a reception to celebrate the twenty-fifth anniversary of one of the journals to which we are both contributors. We fell into a spirited conversation during which Billy

asked me if this reception wasn't the most boring thing I had
ever been to. I said it wasn't, by a long shot. Billy said: "I can't
stand these things where you have to stand up and be civilized.
People either yawn, itch, or drool when they get bored. Which
do you do?"

I said I yawned.

"Huh," said Billy. "You don't look much like a drooler. Let's
get out of here."

This particular interchange is always brought up when inten-
tionality is discussed: Did she mean to pick me up? Did I look
available? And so on. Out on the street we revealed that we
were married and that both of our spouses were out of town.
Having made this clear, we went out to dinner and talked shop.

After dinner Billy said why didn't I come have a drink or a
cup of tea. I did not know what to make of this invitation. I
remembered that the young are more casual about these things,
and that a cup of tea probably meant a cup of tea. My reactions
to this offer are also discussed when cause is under discussion:
Did I want her to seduce me? Did I mean to seduce her? Did we
know what would happen right from the start?

Of her house Billy said: "We don't have good taste or bad
taste. We have no taste." Her living room had no style whatsoever, but it was comfortable enough. There was a portrait of
what looked like an ancestor over the fireplace. Otherwise it
was not a room that revealed a thing about its occupants except
solidity, and a lack of decorative inspiration. Billy made us each
a cup of tea. We continued our conversation, and when Billy
began to look sleepy, I left.

After that, we made a pass at social life. We invited them
for dinner, along with some financial types, a painter, and our
sons and their lady friends. At this gathering Billy was mute,
and Grey, a very clever fellow, chatted interestingly. Billy did
not seem at all comfortable, but the rest of us had a fairly good

time. Then they invited us, along with some financial types they knew and a music critic and his book designer wife. At this dinner, Billy looked tired. It was clear that cooking bothered her. She told me later that she was the sort who, when forced to entertain, did every little thing, like making and straining the veal stock. From the moment she entered the kitchen she looked longingly forward to the time when all the dishes would be clean and put away and the guests would all have gone home.

Then we invited them, but Grey had a bad cold and they had to cancel. After that, Billy and I ran into one another one day when we were both dropping off articles at the same journal and we had lunch. She said she was looking for an article of mine—we had been sending each other articles right from the start. Two days later, after rummaging around in my files, I found it. Since I was going to be in her neighborhood, I dropped it off. She wrote me a note about this article and I called her to discuss it further. This necessitated a lunch meeting. Then she said she was sending me a book I had said I wanted to read, and then I sent her a book, and so it went.

One evening I stopped by to have a chat with Billy and Grey. I had just taken Vera, who was off to California, to the airport. I decided to ring their bell unannounced, but when I got there it turned out that Grey was out of town, too. Had I secretly been hoping that this would be the case? Billy had been working in her study, and without thinking about it, she led me up the stairs. I followed her and at the door of her study, I kissed her. She kissed me right back and looked awful about it.

"Nothing but a kiss!" I said, rather frantically. My mistress was silent. "A friendly kiss," I said.

My mistress gave me the sort of look that is supposed to make your blood freeze, and said: "Is this the way you habitually kiss your friends?"

"It won't happen again," I said. "It was all a mistake."

Billy gave me a stare so bleak and hard that I had no choice but to kiss her again and again.

After all this time it is still impossible for me to figure out what was and is going on in Billy's life that has let me in it. She once remarked that in her opinion there is frequently too little kissing in marriage, through which frail pinprick a microscopic dot of light was thrown on the subject of her marriage—or was it? She is like a Red Indian and says nothing at all, nor does she ever slip.

I, however, do slip, and I am made aware of this by the grim, sidelong glance I am given. I once told Billy that, until I met her, I had never given kissing much thought—she is an insatiable kisser for an unsentimental person—and I was rewarded for this utterance by a well-raised eyebrow and a rather frightening look of registration.

From time to time I feel it is wise to tell Billy how well Vera and I get along.

"Swell," says Billy. "I'm thrilled for you."

"Well, it's true," I say.

"I'm sure it's true," says Billy. "I'm sure there's no reason in the world why you come and see me all the time. It's probably just an involuntary action, like sneezing."

"But you don't understand," I say. "Vera has men friends. I have women friends. The first principle of a good marriage is freedom."

"Oh, I see," says Billy. "You sleep with your other women friends in the morning and come over here in the afternoon. What a lot of stamina you have, for an older person."

One day this conversation had unexpected results. I said how well Vera and I got along, and Billy looked unadornedly hurt.

"God hates a mingy lover," she said. "Why don't you just

say that you're in love with me and that it frightens you and have done with it?"

A lump rose in my throat.

"Of course, maybe you're not in love with me," said Billy in her flattest voice.

I said: "I *am* in love with you."

"Well, there you are," said Billy.

My curiosity about Grey is a huge, violent dog on a very tight leash. He is three years older than Billy, a somewhat sweet-looking boy with rumpled hair who looks as if he is working out problems in higher math as you talk to him. He wears wire-rimmed glasses and his shirttail hangs out. He has the body of a young boy and the air of a genius or someone constantly pre-occupied by the intense pressure of a rarefied mental life. To-gether he and Billy look not so much like husband and wife as co-conspirators.

What are her feelings about him? I begin preliminary queries by hemming and hawing. "Umm," I say, "it's, um, it's a little hard for me to picture your life with Grey. I mean, it's hard to picture your everyday life."

"What you want to know is how often we sleep together and how much do I like it," says Billy.

Well, she has me there, because that is exactly what I want to know.

"Tell you what," says my mistress. "Since you're so forth-coming about *your* marriage, we'll write down all about our home lives on little slips of paper and then we'll exchange them. How's that?"

Well, she has me there, too. What we are doing in each other's lives is a well-tended mystery.

I know how she contrasts to my wife: my wife is affable, full of conversation, loves a dinner party, and is interested in clothes, food, home decor, and the issues of the day. She loves to entertain, is sought out in times of crisis by her numerous friends, and has a kind or original word for everyone. She is methodical, hardworking, and does not fall asleep in restaurants. How I contrast to Grey is another matter, a matter about which I know nothing. I am considerably older and perhaps I appeal to some father longing in my mistress. Billy says Grey is a genius—a thrilling quality but not one that has any real relevance to life with another person. He wishes, according to his wife, that he were the conductor of a symphony orchestra and for this reason he is given musical scores, tickets, and batons for his birthday. He has studied Russian and can sing Russian songs. He is passionately interested in the natural sciences and also wishes he were a forest ranger.

"He sounds so charming," I say, "that I can't imagine why you would want to know someone like me." Billy's response to this is pure silence.

I hunt for signs of him on Billy—jewelry, marks, phrases. I know that he reads astronomy books for pleasure, enjoys cross-country skiing, and likes to travel. Billy says she loves him, but she also says she loves to read the works of Cardinal Aidan Gasquet, the historian of monastic life.

"If you love him so much," I say, taking a page from her book, "why are you hanging around with me?"

"Hanging around," repeats Billy in a bored monotone.

"Well?"

"I am large and contain multitudes," she says, quoting a line from Walt Whitman.

This particular conversation took place en route to a cottage in Vermont which I had rented for five days when both Grey and Vera happened to be out of town at the same time on business.

I remember clearly with what happy anticipation I presented the idea of this cottage to her.

"Guess what?" I said.

"You're pregnant," said Billy.

"I have rented a little cottage for us, in Vermont. For a week when Grey and Vera are away on their long trips. We can go there and watch the leaves turn."

"The leaves have already turned and fallen off," said Billy faintly. She looked away and didn't speak for some time.

"We don't have to go, Billy," I said. "I only sent the check yesterday. I can cancel it."

There appeared to be tears in my mistress' eyes.

"No," she said. "Don't do that. I'll split it with you."

"You don't seem pleased," I said.

"Being pleased doesn't strike me as the appropriate response to the idea of sneaking off to a love nest with your lover," said Billy.

"What *is* the appropriate response?" I said.

"Oh," Billy said, her voice now blithe, "sorrow, guilt, horror, anticipation."

Well, she can run but she can't hide. My mistress is given away from time to time by her own expressions. No matter how hard she tries to suppress the visible evidence of what she feels, she is not always successful. Her eyes turn color, becoming dark and rather smoky. This is as good as a plain declaration of love. Billy's mental life, her grumpiness, her irritability, her crotchets are like static that, from time to time, give way to a clear signal, just as you often hit a pure band of music on a car radio after turning the dial through a lot of chaotic squawk.

In French movies of a certain period, the lovers are seen leaving the woman's apartment or house. His car is parked on an attractive side street. She is carrying a leather valise and is wearing a silk scarf around her neck. He is carrying the wicker basket she has packed with their picnic lunch. They will have the sort of food lovers have for lunch in these movies: a roasted chicken, a bottle of champagne, and a goat cheese wrapped up in leaves. Needless to say, when Billy and I finally left to go to our love nest, no such sight presented itself to me. First of all, she met me around the corner from my garage after a number of squabbles about whose car to take. She was standing between a rent-a-car and an animal hospital, wearing an old skirt, her old jacket, and carrying a ratty canvas overnight bag. No lacy underwear would be drawn from it, I knew. My mistress buys her white cotton undergarments at the five-and-ten-cent store. She wears an old T-shirt of Grey's to sleep in, she tells me.

For lunch we had hamburgers—no romantic rural inn or picnic spot for us—at Hud's Burger Hut off the thruway.

As we drew closer to our destination, Billy began to fidget, reminding me that having her along was sometimes not unlike traveling with a small child.

In the town nearest our love nest we stopped and bought coffee, milk, sugar, and cornflakes. Because I am a domestic animal and not a mere savage, I remembered to buy bread, butter, cheese, salami, eggs, and a number of cans of tomato soup.

Billy surveyed these items with a raised eyebrow.

"This is the sort of stuff you buy when you intend to stay indoors and kick up a storm of passion," she said.

It was an off-year Election Day—congressional and Senate races were being run. We had both voted, in fact, before taking off. Our love nest had a radio which I instantly switched on to hear if there were any early returns while we gave the place a cursory glance and put the groceries away. Then we flung ourselves onto the unmade bed, for which I had thoughtfully remembered to pack sheets.

When our storm of passion had subsided, my mistress stared impassively at the ceiling.

"In bed with Frank and Billy," she intoned. "It was Election Day, and Frank and Billy were once again in bed. Election returns meant nothing to them. The future of their great nation was inconsequential, so busy were they flinging themselves at one another they could barely be expected to think for one second of any larger issues. The subjects to which these trained economists could have spoken, such as inflationary spirals or deficit budgeting, were as mere dust."

"Shut up, Billy," I said.

She did shut up. She put on my shirt and went off to the kitchen. When she returned she had two cups of coffee and a plate of toasted cheese on a tray. With the exception of her dinner party, this was the first meal I had ever had at her hands.

"I'm starving," she said, getting under the covers. We polished off our snack, propped up with pillows. I asked Billy if she might like a second cup of coffee and she gave me a look of remorse and desire that made my head spin.

"Maybe you wanted to go out to dinner," she said. "You like a proper dinner." Then she burst into tears. "I'm sorry," she said. These were words I had never heard her speak before.

"Sorry?" I said. "Sorry for what?"

"I didn't ask you what you wanted to do," my mistress said. "You might have wanted to take a walk, or go for a drive or look around the house or make the bed."

I stared at her.

"I don't want a second cup of coffee," Billy said. "Do you?"

I got her drift and did not get out of bed. The forthrightness of her desire for me melted my heart.

During this excursion, none of my expectations came to pass. We did not, for example, have long talks about our respective marriages or our future together or apart. We did not discover what our domestic life might be like. We lived like graduate students or mice and not like normal people at all. We kept odd hours and lived off sandwiches. We stayed in bed and were both glad when it rained. When the sun came out, we went for a walk and observed the bare and almost bare trees. From time to time I would switch on the radio to hear the latest election results and commentary.

"Because of this historic time," Billy said, "you will never be able to forget me. It is a rule of life that care must be taken in choosing whom one will be in bed with during Great Moments in History. You are now stuck, with me and this week of important congressional elections twined in your mind forever."

It was in the car on the way home that the subject of what we were doing together came up. It was twilight and we had both been silent.

"This is the end of the line," said Billy.

"What do you mean?" I said. "Do you mean you want to break this up?"

"No," said Billy. "It would be nice, though, wouldn't it?"

"No, it would not be nice," I said.

"I think it would," said Billy. "Then I wouldn't spend all my time wondering what we are doing together when I could be thinking about other things, like my dissertation."

"What do you think we are doing together?" I said.

"It's simple," said Billy. "Some people have dogs or kitty cats. You're my pet."

"Come on."

"Okay, you're right. Those are only child substitutes. You're my child substitute until I can make up my mind about having a child."

At this, my blood freezes. Whose child does she want to have?

Every now and then when overcome with tenderness—on those occasions naked, carried away, and looking at one another with sweetness in our eyes—my mistress and I smile dreamily and realize that if we dwelt together for more than a few days, in the real world and not in some love nest, we would soon learn to hate each other. It would never work. We both know it. She is too relentlessly dour, and too fond of silence. I prefer false cheer to no cheer and I like conversation over dinner no matter what. Furthermore we would never have proper meals and, although I cannot cook, I like to dine. I would soon resent her lack of interest in domestic arrangements and she would resent me for resenting her. Furthermore, Billy is a slob. She does not leave towels lying on the bathroom floor, but she throws them over the shower curtain rod any old way instead of folding them or hanging them properly so they can dry. It is things like this that squash out romance over a period of time.

As for Billy, she often sneers at me. She finds many of my opinions quaint. She thinks I am an old-time domestic fascist. She refers to me as "an old-style heterosexual throwback" or "old hetero" because I like to pay for dinner, open car doors, and often call her at night when Grey is out of town to make sure she is safe. The day the plumber came to fix a leak in her sink, I called several times.

"He's gone," Billy said. "And he left big, greasy paw prints all over me." She found this funny, I did not.

After a while, were we to cohabit, I believe I would be driven nuts and she would come to loathe me. My household is well run and well regulated. I like routine and I like things to go along smoothly. We employ a flawless person by the name of Mrs. Ivy Castle who has been flawlessly running our house for years. She is an excellent housekeeper and a marvelous cook. Our relations with her are formal.

The Delielles employ a feckless person called Mimi-Ann Browning who comes in once a week to push the dust around. Mimi-Ann hates routines and schedules, and is constantly changing the days of the people she works for. It is quite something to hear Billy on the telephone with her.

"Oh, Mimi-Ann," she will say. "Please don't switch me. I beg you. Grey's awful cousin is coming and the house is really disgusting. Please, Mimi. I'll do anything. I'll do your mother-in-law's tax return. I'll be your eternal slave. *Please.* Oh, thank you, Mimi-Ann. Thank you a million times."

Now why, I ask myself, does my mistress never speak to me like that?

In the sad twilight on the way home from our week together, I asked myself, as I am always asking myself: could I exist in some ugly flat with my cheerless mistress? I could not, as my mistress is always the first to point out.

She said that the small doses we got of one another made it possible for us to have a love affair but that a taste of ordinary life would do us in. She correctly pointed out that our only common interest was each other, since we had such vast differences of opinion on the subject of economics. Furthermore, we were not simply lovers, nor were we mere friends, and since we were not going to end up together, there was nothing for it.

I was silent.

"Face it," said my tireless mistress. "We have no raison d'être."

There was no disputing this.

I said: "If we have no raison d'être, Billy, then what are we to do?"

These conversations flare up like tropical storms. The climate is always right for them. It is simply a question of when they will occur.

"Well?" I said.

"I don't know," said my mistress, who generally has a snappy answer for everything. A wave of fatherly affection and worry came over me. I said, in a voice so drenched with concern it caused my mistress to scowl like a child about to receive an injection: "Perhaps you should think about this more seriously, Billy. You and Grey are really just starting out. Vera and I have been married a long, long time. I think I am more a disruption in your life than you are in mine."

"Oh, really," said Billy.

"Perhaps we should see each other less," I said. "Perhaps we should part."

"Okay, let's part," said Billy. "You go first." Her face was set and I entertained myself with the notion that she was trying not to burst into tears. Then she said: "What are you going to do all day after we part?"

This was not a subject to which I wanted to give much thought.

"Isn't our raison d'être that we're fond of one another?" I said. "I'm awfully fond of you."

"Gee, that's interesting," Billy said. "Just last week you broke down and used the word 'love.' How quickly things change."

"You know what I mean."

"Whatever our status quos are," Billy said, "they are being maintained like mad."

This silenced me. Billy and I have the world right in place. Nothing flutters, changes, or moves. Whatever is being preserved in our lives is safely preserved. It is quite true, as Billy, who believes in function, points out, that we are in each other's life for a reason, but neither of us will state the reason. Nevertheless, although there are some cases in which love is not a good or sufficient reason for anything, the fact is, love is undeniable.

Yes, love is undeniable and that is the tricky point. It is one of the sobering realizations of adult life that love is often not a propellant. Thus, in those romantic movies, the tender mistress stays married to her stuffy husband—the one with the mustache and the stiff tweeds—while the lover is seen walking through the countryside with his long-suffering wife and faithful dog. It often seems that the function of romance is to give people something romantic to think about.

The question is: if it is true, as my mistress says, that she is going to stay with Grey and I am going to stay with Vera, why is it that we are together every chance we get?

There was, of course, an explanation for this, and my indefatigable mistress came up with it, God bless her.

"It's an artistic impulse," she said. "It takes us out of reality and gives us an invented context all our own."

"Oh, I see," I said. "It's only art."

"Don't get in a huff," Billy said. "We're in a very unusual situation. It has to do with limited doting, restricted thrall, and situational adoration."

"Oh, how interesting," I said. "Are doting, thrall, and adoration things you actually feel for me?"

Naturally Billy would never deign to answer a leading question.

Every adult knows that facts must be faced. In adult life, it often seems that's all there is. Prior to our weekend together, the unguarded moments between us had been kept to a minimum. Now they came more frequently. That week together haunted us. It dogged our heels. It made us long for and dread—what an unfortunate combination!—each other.

One evening I revealed to her how I sometimes feel as I watch her walk up the stairs to the door of her house. I feel she is walking into her real and still fairly young life. She will leave me in the dust, I think. I think of all the things that have not yet happened to her, that have not yet gone wrong, and I think of her life with Grey, which is still fairly unlived.

One afternoon she told me how it makes her feel when she thinks of my family table—with Vera and our sons and their friends and girl friends, of our years of shared meals, of all that lived life. Billy described this feeling as a band around her head and a hot pressure in the area of her heart. I, of course, merely get a lump in my throat. Why do these admittings take place at twilight or at dusk, in the gloomiest light when everything looks dirty, eerie, faded, or inevitable?

Our conversation comes to a dead halt, like a horse balking before a hurdle, on the issue of what we want. I have tried my best to formulate what it is I want from Billy, but I have not gotten very far. Painful consideration has brought forth this revelation: I want her not ever to stop being. This is as close as grammar or reflection will allow.

One day the horse will jump over the hurdle and the end will come. The door will close. Billy will doubtless do the closing. She will decide she wants a baby, or Grey will be offered an academic post in London, or Billy will finish her dissertation and get a job in Boston, and the Delielles will move. Or perhaps Vera will come home one evening and say that she longs to live in Paris or San Francisco, and we will move. What will happen then?

Perhaps my mistress is right. A love affair is like a work of art. The large store of reference and jokes, the history of our friendship, our trip to Vermont, our numberless phone calls, this edifice, this monument, this civilization known only to and constructed by the two of us will be—what will it be? Billy once read me an article from one of Grey's nature magazines about the last Coast Salish Indian to speak Wintu. All the others of his tribe were dead. That is how I would feel, deprived of Billy.

The awful day will doubtless come. It is like thinking about the inevitability of nuclear war. But for now, I continue to ring her doorbell. Her greeting is delivered in a bored monotone. "Oh, it's you," she will say.

I will follow her upstairs to her study and there we will hurl ourselves at one another. I will reflect, as I always do, how very bare the setting for these encounters is. Not a picture on the wall, not an ornament. Even the quilt that keeps the chill off us on the couch is faded.

In one of her snootier moments, my mistress said to me: "My furnishings are interior. I care about what I think about."

As I gather her into my arms, I cannot help imagining all that interior furniture, those hard-edged things she thinks about, whatever is behind her silence, whatever, in fact, her real story is.

I imagine that some day she will turn to me and with some tone in her voice I have never heard before say: "We can't see each other any more." We will both know the end has come. But meanwhile she is right close by. After a fashion, she is mine. I watch her closely to catch the look of true love that every once in a while overtakes her. She knows I am watching, and she knows the effect her look has. "A baby could take candy from you," she says.

Our feelings have edges and spines and prickles like a cactus, or porcupine. Our parting when it comes will not be simple, either. Depicted it would look like one of those medieval beasts that have fins, fur, scales, feathers, claws, wings, and horns. In a world apart from anyone else, we are Frank and Billy, with no significance to anyone but the other. Oh, the terrible privacy and loneliness of love affairs!

Under the quilt with our arms interlocked, I look into my mistress' eyes. They are dark, and full of concealed feeling. If we hold each other close enough, that darkness is held at bay. The mission of the lover is, after all, to love. I can look at Billy and see clear back to the first time we met, to our hundreds of days together, to her throwing the towels over the shower curtain rod, to each of her gestures and intonations. She is the road I have traveled to her, and I am hers.

Oh, Billy! Oh, art! Oh, memory!

Frank and Billy

At a perfectly ordinary cocktail party given by the *Journal of American Economic Thought* for its staff and contributors, Francis Clemens was introduced to the author of some articles he had admired on the subject of medieval capitalism. Her name was Josephine Delielle (nicknamed Billy) and although it slipped right by him at the time, he fell in love with her at once.

She had lank brown hair, gray-blue eyes, and a deadpan mug. Her expression ranged from a frown to a somewhat grudging grin.

"Oh, how nice to meet you," Billy said. "You had an article in last month's issue. Aren't you the guy who writes about economics and architecture?"

Francis noticed that her bottom teeth were slightly crooked, and asked her what she had thought about this article.

"I thought it was a little goofy," she said. Francis surveyed her further and saw that her shirttail was hanging out on the side.

"Oh, yes?" Francis said. "Which parts did you find especially goofy?"

In the ensuing conversation, it was made clear to Francis that she found all or most of his article goofy. She explained why she felt this way, and then she said: "Don't you think this is the most boring thing you've ever been to?"

"Not by a long shot," Francis said. "But then I'm considerably older than you."

Billy gave him a hard stare—the look of an appraiser at a diamond. This clear, naked child-gaze of hers made it difficult for Francis to guess how old she was. These days it was hard for Francis to tell how old most women were, and Billy could have been anywhere from twenty-five to thirty-nine. She looked older than his oldest son's girl friend, who was twenty-six, but younger than his wife Vera's partner in her interior design business, who was forty-two.

Billy was speaking, but Francis's attention had wandered. He felt a kind of inward lurch, as if he were having a dream about falling off a ledge. The air in his chest felt sweet as it does after a long laugh or when a headache has finally gone away. He felt as if he and Billy were standing in thick hazy sunshine. He heard the word "husband." Her husband, Grey Delielle, was at a conference in Switzerland—he was the economic adviser to a small foundation. Francis had heard of this foundation and his head cleared further. Vera was in San Diego redoing a beach house. It occurred to him that Billy might be lonely for company at dinner. He suggested they leave the party and go off to a restaurant.

"Swell," she said, and they went to get their coats.

At dinner Francis discovered that Billy taught two classes a week at the business school, and Billy discovered that Francis had resigned from his banking firm several years ago and now consulted to clients on the telephone. He was also writing a book on the relationship of architectural and financial trends. Billy revealed that she was working on her dissertation, the subject of which was the effect of the medieval wool trade on a Cotswold village. A long conversation about English architecture ensued.

Francis spoke a little about his wife, Vera—Billy must meet her—and his two grown sons, Quentin and Aaron. Billy said that Grey, her husband, was sort of a genius but she did not say that Francis must meet him.

It was a lovely night in early May. Francis walked Billy home. She and Grey lived on two floors of a brownstone into which Billy invited Francis for a drink or cup of tea. He asked for tea and it was several months before he realized that he had chosen it over the drink he really wanted because its preparation might keep him with Billy for a few minutes more. He also realized that one of the reasons he had found her living room so ugly was that it is perfectly normal for the lover to hate his or her beloved's place of legal and habitual residence.

Francis did not know that he was embarking on a love affair. He went home and slept peacefully, after making himself a strong, bracing drink. In the morning he remembered Billy's saying that she had been looking for a certain book, a book he owned. He dispatched it to her at once, and she responded by sending him an article *he* had mentioned which she happened to have in her files. They met, not entirely by chance, at the *Journal* office. It was just around lunchtime and so they went around the corner for a sandwich. A week later Francis just happened to be near the business school and he just happened to bump into Billy after her class.

After several months of meetings and luncheons, Francis became familiar with Billy's uninspired wardrobe and her array of faded sweatshirts, shapeless turtlenecks, and worn corduroy skirts and frayed boys' shirts.

One day he said, looking at her brother's old sweater and a skirt that might once have been olive green: "You're the one girl, Billy, whom you dread to hear say: I'm going to slip into something more comfortable."

It was clearly provocative, and not at all the sort of thing Francis was used to saying. Billy did not bat an eyelash. She put down her pastrami sandwich, wiped her lips with a paper napkin, and said: "No one my age ever says anything like that. We just take our clothes off."

A long while later she revealed that she had said this to hurt him, and he did not think it wise to tell her how effective she had been.

It was months before he kissed her, and by that time the idea of kissing her had turned into an overwhelming desire he was tired of fending off. Reluctantly he came to the conclusion that he was simply looking for an opportunity.

One evening, after taking Vera to the airport on another of her trips to San Diego, a terrible restlessness took possession of him. The idea of going to a movie or going home to his empty house made him more restless than ever. It could have been said that he was looking for action, but that phrase was not in his working vocabulary. He drove into Manhattan in an agitated state until it occurred to him that he might very well pay a call on that charming young couple Billy and Grey Delielle. They were doubtless at home—Francis had heard Billy say many times that there was no hell more hellish than the hell of social life. She did not like to go out, and she did not like to entertain, either. It was not very late. Francis could easily just stop by, although just stopping by was not the sort of thing he generally did.

On the other hand, the Delielles might be ready for bed.

They might in fact *be* in bed—a terrible thought. As he neared their neighborhood he wondered what he would do if in fact they were out. He felt it was possible that he might have a fit.

He found a parking space directly in front of their brownstone, bounded up the stairs, and rang the bell.

Billy answered the door, wearing blue jeans and a pair of tasseled loafers that had seen so many, many better days that they were kept together with a variety of duct and electrical tapes. She did not seem surprised to see him. Rather a kind of impish smirk overtook her usually expressionless features. It was almost plain to see that she was repressing a smile.

"I was right around the corner," Francis lied. "At a very boring dinner party. I don't generally drop by, but I was right in the neighborhood."

"Oh," said Billy.

"I hope I'm not dropping by at a bad time. I mean, you and Grey might have already turned in." Francis felt his scalp begin to prickle.

"Grey's in Chicago," said Billy. "I was working. Come in and I'll give you a drink."

But she did not go toward the kitchen. Absentmindedly she wandered up the stairs toward her study. Francis followed her. His heart was beating wildly. The bedroom and the guest room were also upstairs, he knew. Where was she taking him?

He had forgotten how these things are accomplished. Did one grab the girl by the arm, or tackle her by the ankle? Did one pluck at the sleeve of her turtleneck, tap her on the back? Ask? Beg?

Of course Francis had forgotten that in the case of true love, things simply happen—almost the only circumstances under which they do. People just look at each other in a certain way, and the signal is as unmistakable as the mating behavior of Atwater's prairie chicken.

What happened was that Billy got to the door of her study and then turned around, clearly confused. Only later did Francis realize that she had no idea of what she was doing. She looked at him with a puzzled, unfocused aspect that was totally out of character for her.

"What am I doing up here?" she said. "I was supposed to make you a drink."

She looked up at him, and he looked down at her. The realization that he had fallen in love caused his heart first to shrink and then to expand.

Billy took a step toward the stair which only moved her a step closer to Francis. His chin, he saw, would graze her head. One more step in either direction—she toward him, or he toward her—and they were in each other's arms. Francis felt impelled to move: he felt in the grip of a great many involuntary actions. His hand was on her shoulder. It was on her back. His other arm encircled her. He pulled her close. Some other hand —it had to have been his right or left—entangled its fingers in her hair and tipped her head back. Francis felt her arms slowly creep up his sides and around his neck in a gesture that was either tender or grudging. To his amazement he saw that Billy's eyes were closed. She looked soft and dreamy—quite unlike her usual exasperated self. He was about to kiss her when she opened her eyes. These eyes, generally a hard, unavailing, unsentimental blue-gray, the sort of eyes that see right through a thing, had turned, it seemed to him, one shade darker. Francis felt very like a swimmer about to jump into a deep pool of cold water. It was now or never. He pulled her close again. Their lips met.

Hers were soft, and tasted of raspberries. Her hair smelled of baby shampoo.

Of course, first kisses tell it all. They reveal, as it were, the inner man. Billy's first responses were tentative and noncommittal—as noncommittal as you can be wrapped up in someone else's arms. She *was* grudging, and Francis knew that she would always be. But when she really kissed him back, he learned that she felt about him as he felt about her, although he knew it would be rather like breaking rocks ever to get her to say it. He would never hear a whispered endearment from her lips, he was certain. As for Francis, even he knew what he was broadcasting. Relief, guilt, and liberation made him passionate. He was hers entirely, after a manner of speaking.

Their first actual kiss was a one-celled organism which, after they had been standing on the stairway kissing for some time, evolved into something rather grander—a bird of paradise, for example. Francis was afraid to stop kissing her. He feared that she might vanish as smoke, or throw herself against the wall and accuse him of being a cad, or she might sob out Grey's name and fling herself down the stairs. But he longed to look at her to see what effect, if any, all this kissing had on her. He took her very firmly by the arms so that she could not vanish or fling, but he was unable to read her expression because she was staring at the floor. This made him angry and he shook her ever so slightly. When she did look up, there was so much on her face he hardly knew where to begin. She looked confused, en-raptured, upset, and stunned. He saw desire, despair, elation, surprise, mistrust, and longing. So that was what her determined expressionlessness concealed!

She looked up and uttered two words.

"Oh, more," she said, and this time she put her arms around him. Francis's heart melted with gratitude. It was one thing to be in love. It was quite another to be loved back. Francis kissed her and kissed her. They kissed with their eyes closed, like teen-agers. Finally Billy pushed herself away. She looked disarranged and upset. Any fool, after all, knows that two adults cannot stand around kissing endlessly. Decisions of one sort or another usually present themselves for immediate attention.

"Enough of this nonsense," Billy said in an unsteady voice.

"I wish you'd stop staring at the floor," said Francis. "It's very disconcerting."

"I can't look at you," Billy said. "It's too dangerous."

At this a smile overtook him—a smile of triumph. He pulled her close again.

"This doesn't have to happen ever again," Francis said, lying through his teeth.

"Interesting," said Billy, "if true." With this she slid against him as easily as people slide against each other in a swimming pool and in a very few minutes the decision was made to repair to Billy's unattractive little study, where, on her threadbare and faded couch, they discovered how ardently and secretly they had waited for one another.

The first kiss is a snap. It is the aftermath of the first real connection that produces such a mire of unwanted feelings. Billy sat up. The faded quilt she had pulled over them to keep off the chill slipped away. Francis noticed that without her clothes she looked quite chic, unlike most people, who look more stylish when dressed. Perhaps, he thought, it was the contrast between her nice body and her awful clothes.

Billy stared at the wall, then pushed the hair out of her eyes and scowled her exasperated frown. It was a gesture which by now Francis had seen dozens of times.

"Gee, I feel awful," she said.

"Oh, do you?" said Francis fiercely. He pulled her down, and quickly established that she did not feel quite so awful as she said. Their hunger for one another was quite startling—a subject Francis felt would never be discussed.

Francis did not know what to expect in the way of an aftermath. He had never had a real love affair before. He had had romances; he had gotten married; and from time to time he had found himself in bed with some old friend or other—nothing serious at all: it wasn't romance so much as social service or cheering someone up. Next to him Billy lay with her arms crossed on her chest, looking at the ceiling like a child filled with some secret, inner amusement.

"In bed with Frank and Billy," she began. "Chapter one. Frank and Billy have just gone to bed. They have been in bed for who can say how long. Doubtless they will go to bed again, and the funny thing is, they're both married, and to other people! What a situation. How long, they might ask, has this been going on? Who will ask first?"

"How long has this been going on?" Francis said.

"That wasn't necessarily a cue," Billy said, and silence fell between them.

Instead, Francis watched his beloved begin to get dressed. As she slipped her clothes over her head, he realized how considerably less gorgeous she was making herself. When she pulled on her tatty corduroys, he saw before him the old recognizable Billy, who like the strange, unclothed Billy was also his.

When she put on her shoes Francis felt it was time for him to get dressed, too. He looked at the clock. "Good Lord," he said. "We've been on this couch for two and a half hours."

Billy gave him a look he could not interpret. Did it mean that two and a half hours was a very long time, or not a very long time by her lights?

As he put his shirt on, he noticed that some of her mild, sweet smell seemed to have rubbed off on him. He was terribly happy —as happy as it is possible to be under these circumstances, which bring the kind of happiness that is devoid of any contentment.

It was quite amazing, he thought, that such a welter of complex feeling can arise from the simplest things—the sight of a shirttail hanging out. He had wanted to kiss that deadpan mug's face the instant he had seen it, he now admitted.

Billy folded up the quilt. The couch looked as if no one had

ever so much as sat upon it. Reality set in, cold as a fog. Vera
would have landed in San Diego by now and would be calling
in if she had not already done so. How lovely it would be to
live in a movie in which lovers have only time, not the telephone calls of absent spouses to worry about. But what about
Billy? Did she expect him to stay? Oh, how complicated these
things were!

"Do you want a cup of tea before you leave?" Billy said,
standing at the door.

"Are you so anxious to get rid of me?" asked Francis. He was
relieved and sad. The fact that he would soon leave set him free.

"You weren't thinking of sleeping over, were you?" said
Billy, shocked. She looked about fifteen years old.

Downstairs Francis sat on a stool in Billy's kitchen while she
boiled the water for tea. In novels, Francis reflected, lovers in-
dulge in some form of afterglow: they beam at one another or
smile radiant smiles. It was very clear that only the remotest
afterglow was going to envelop him and Billy, but as he watched
her set out the cups, his heart began to ache. She looked small
in her big serious-looking kitchen, and he knew because she had
told him how much she hated to cook. He wondered where she
truly belonged. And where did he belong? How torn he felt by
his own joy at where he was sitting and the terrible strangeness
of sitting there!

No one, he reflected sadly, ever possesses anyone else. The
act of love can be performed by complete strangers, but it is
quite another thing to have access to what someone else actually
thinks. Even though they were officially lovers, Francis felt himself tongue-tied and confused. He grabbed her by the arm as
she walked by him. He spun her around hard and pressed her
to him.

"I'm in love with you," he said.

"I know," Billy said.

"Well, what about you?" said Francis. "Or do you always sleep with people when Grey is out of town?"

"Geez," Billy said. "What's wrong with you, anyway?"

"You told me you young people just take your clothes off."

Billy gave him a baleful look.

"I guess I'm a desperate man," Francis said.

"Oh, pish," Billy said. "Why don't you just ask me instead of filling the air with innuendo?"

"All right," Francis said. "Are you in love with me?"

"Sure," said Billy. After a long pause, she said, "Watch out. The water's boiling right behind you."

With these words was Francis's heart set at ease.

Francis was a thoroughly married man, and had been for many years. He thought like a married person and therefore the aftermath of his evening with Billy filled him with guilt and glee. He did not know what he felt worse about—the guilt or the glee. They existed in equal measure, along with a number of other things he had not felt in quite a long time: he was as excited, hopeful, and confused as a teenaged boy. He was also extremely tired. He made himself a drink and thought he might take a bath, but instead he crawled into bed quite aware of the fact that he did not want to wash the evening off himself so quickly.

Francis had not slept alone very much in his adult life, but now that Vera traveled for her work, he found that he rather liked being in bed by himself. The bed they shared was enormous—and was covered, due to Vera's domestic genius and connections in the world of decoration, with a blue and white coverlet of early American design homespun by a weaver in

Vermont who specialized in reproductions. It was possibly the largest blue and white coverlet of its kind in the world.

He sipped his drink and tried to make his mind a perfect blank, but the image of Billy in many guises darted through his tired brain. He looked over at Vera's side of the bed and imagined Billy in it. Vera wore linen shifts to bed and piled her hair on top of her head to sleep. She slept like a kitten and smelled of Rose Bleue. Billy, he imagined, slept in a rotten-looking flannel nightgown. How he wished she were next to him!

He dozed off, calculating that he had five days until Vera returned, and five hours until he could call up his grouchy girl friend and hear her voice again.

That had been in the spring. It was now October. On a sultry, hazy day, Francis drove to Billy's. She said she thought they ought to have a serious talk. Two blocks from her house, he was confronted by the sight of his beloved mistress struggling under a load of men's suits in plastic bags—Grey's suits which she was fetching from the cleaners. It was hot and Billy looked sweaty and cross. These were doubtless Grey's fall and winter suits coming out of storage in time for Grey's trip to Switzerland. This trip was of consuming interest to Francis as Vera was due to go to Honolulu at the same time, and it was his single-minded desire to take Billy away with him somewhere for a few days to find out what, if anything, she wore in bed.

It occurred to him to stop the car and help her, but this seemed to him an ambiguous gesture, and so he drove on. Did Grey, that swine, expect Billy to run these errands for him? Or did she do it out of love? He gave her time to get home, and when he drove up her street he found her again, this time with a bundle of laundry. She was taking Grey's shirts and the sheets to be laundered. This time she saw him and hopped into the car.

Why, he wondered, did he always have to see her carrying such intimate bundles?

Francis drove her to the laundry and then followed her into her living room where, he supposed, this serious talk was about to begin. But he was wrong. The sky darkened and lightning flashed directly overhead. It began to pour. Billy sprang up. "I left the windows open," she said, and dashed up the stairs.

Francis followed. She banged down the windows in her study and then went into the bedroom. Francis had looked into this room many times but he had never actually been in it.

Of course, the lover's nuptial couch is an object of horrible fascination. The lover is drawn to it, drawn to lie down upon it, and drawn to say what a miserable bed it is.

Francis sat down. The bed was a four-poster, high off the ground and not, Francis noted, very wide. It was covered by a pink quilt, which was the nicest thing he had yet seen of Billy's possessions. He stretched out, in a tentative way.

"Jesus," he said. "This is a very hard mattress. Or maybe it isn't a mattress. Maybe it's a plank of wood."

"I have a plank of wood, you have a football field," Billy said, referring to Francis's enormous cot, which she had been shown during a tour of his house. She thought his house was frightful, and said so often. She referred to it as "your charming little snuggery." Francis's house was usually considered to be quite beautiful. Billy said it made her feel as if she was imprisoned inside a tea cozy.

It was amazing how many things prevented Billy and Francis from having their serious conversation. It was put off dozens of times, during which Francis went forward to achieve his heart's desire: he wanted to take Billy on a little trip and sleep the whole night through with her next to him. He saw an ad for a cottage in Vermont and rented it on the spot for five days when Vera and Grey would be away at the same time. This happened very infrequently and not for this long—a whole week. Francis felt this should be taken advantage of. Billy, of course, was mute.

The Sunday before he and Billy were due to leave, Francis put Vera on her plane and began his restless way back into Manhattan. He thought he might take a little drive past Billy's just to see if she was visible. She might be sitting on her front steps, or walking down the street with the Sunday paper.

She was walking down the street, but not with the Sunday papers. She was walking with her very husband, Grey. They were holding hands and laughing. It was not jealousy that lashed against Francis's heart, but anger: she never *told* him that she held Grey's hand or that they ever laughed. His vision of their marriage was a still photo of two people at opposite ends of the table who are silent because they have absolutely nothing whatsoever to say to one another. Francis had always assumed that she and Grey had nothing—nothing in common. It was amazing how exotic they looked to Francis, who was so used to the sight of Billy with him that he could not get over the sight of her with her lawful husband. Of course it was not unknown for Francis to hold Vera's hand, or for them to laugh at the same jokes, but that was quite another thing entirely.

One night in the bedroom of the rented love nest in Vermont, Francis turned to Billy. She was wearing his T-shirt and reading a book. The bed they were lying in was a little smaller than the bed Billy and Grey shared, and it was necessary for Francis and Billy to sleep like bunnies, or spoons or vines.

"Is that what you normally wear to bed?" Francis said.

"Normally I don't wear *your* T-shirt to bed," said Billy.

"Isn't that the one I wore today?" said Francis.

"Uh-huh," Billy said. "I like 'em broken in."

Francis was in a partial swoon. The cottage was drafty and the television didn't work. Now they lay in bed with their separate books. The idea that he was actually in bed with Billy and reading—or pretending to read—made his heart a little wild.

"Sex is a funny thing," he began in a fatherly tone.

"Yes, hilarious," said Billy. "Listen to this." She held up her book. It was entitled *Green Demons*, by someone called Ardith Chase Lamondt. "He drew her to him with a quick intake of breath. The delicate ribs along her spine quivered slightly."

"Yours never do," Francis said.

"You never draw me to you with a quick intake of breath," Billy said. "I tell you, sex in this book is a pretty funny thing. What's your book?" She leaned over and turned his book toward her. "Oh, yick," she said. "I got my book off the shelf in the living room. You actually *packed* yours. I didn't see any books by Important Thinkers in this house. I think it's hilarious that you actually brought a book along to our illicit love nest."

"I wish you wouldn't talk that way," Francis said.

"Oh, come on," Billy said. "Isn't that book the most boring thing you've ever read?"

"This man is very important, miss. If you weren't so smug, you'd read him, too. Besides, a man needs to keep up with his times."

"Huh," said Billy. "Well, I made up an all purpose Important Title for you in the car. I was thinking about your bookshelves and I synthesized all the titles into one Very Important Title. You can use it when people ask you what you're reading and you aren't actually reading anything."

"What's that?" said Francis.

"It's *Towards a Scarcity of Needs*," she said. "I'm ever so proud of it. It has a nice, official sound and it means absolutely nothing at all. It's the right title for a man who goes on an illicit trip and brings a book along, to say nothing of constantly listening to the news on the radio."

Towards a Scarcity of Needs! No one in the world except

Francis and Billy would ever know what this meant. If he ever mentioned it in passing, no one would have the slightest idea what he was talking about.

Having a love affair, Francis reflected, was not unlike being the co-governor of a tiny, private kingdom in some remote country with only two inhabitants—you and the other co-governor. This kingdom had flora and fauna, a national bird, language, reference, conceit, a national anthem (*Towards a Scarcity of Needs*), cheers, songs, and gestures. It also had national censorship—the taboo subjects are taboo. The idea that one of the co-governors has a life outside the kingdom always brings pain. For example, the afternoon Francis's eye fell on a thick air letter in an elderly hand. When pressed, Billy turned red and explained that for many years she had been having a correspondence with a retired schoolteacher in the town of Northleach whom she had met during one of her research periods in the Cotswolds. He sent her hand-knitted mittens of local wool. She sent him new mystery books. They wrote a letter each month. This information left Francis speechless, like a blow to the stomach with a flat object. The moment he stepped out of her house her life without him began. Of course, the same could be said of him.

What richness! what privacy! what sadness!

Suddenly, Francis was exhausted. It had been a long two days: a tiring drive to Vermont, the strangeness of having Billy all to himself with no curfew, their odd and scarce hours of sleep. He leaned against the insufficient pillows. At home he slept with two pillows filled amply with European goosedown.

Life was really very simple. What he wanted to know was this: did Billy love him more than she loved her husband, Grey? On the other hand, life was very complicated. He did not want to know any of the possible answers to this question. His eyelids were heavy but he thought he might rouse himself and ask

Billy some burning question such as: what *are* we doing together?

He turned and there was Billy wearing his T-shirt. Her hair
fell into her eyes, and she brushed it off her face with a drowsy
hand. She was fast asleep, her head full of alien, unknowable
dreams.

French Movie

Billy Delielle sat in her study on a rainy afternoon staring out the window and watching the rain fall in steady sheets. Her papers were spread before her. She was rewriting the third chapter of her dissertation, which was entitled "The Economics of the Medieval Wool Trade in a Cotswold Village."

Three years ago Billy had gotten a study grant which she had spent in a cramped alcove in the Gloucester records office tracing the rising and declining fortunes of shepherds, landowners, weavers, and cloth merchants. Grey timed his vacation with Billy's grant. Together they put up at the Heald Hotel outside of Chipping Camden, where they shared a lumpy bed in a room wallpapered with cabbage roses.

Billy remembered the exact smell of her alcove: dust, old paper, floor wax. She remembered the afternoon hikes she took with Grey and the hours they had spent exploring in their rented car. When her grant expired they drove to Scotland to visit Grey's sister and her family.

These recollections were not sweet to Billy, although that

time had been one of the sweetest in Billy's life. It was disconcerting to be dreaming of a lovely time spent with your husband
when you were, as Billy was, waiting for your lover.

Francis Clemens had taken his wife, Vera, to the airport, and
now Billy was tracking his probable progress back into the city.
Vera was consulting on the construction of a library for handicapped citizens in Seattle. By this time, Billy figured, Francis
would be driving through the Midtown Tunnel and soon enough
would be cruising her block for a parking space.

Billy's previously safe, organized, and tidy life had been
transformed, by the presence of this extraordinary irritant, into
something resembling one of those oddly shaped freshwater
pearls—Billy knew about these because of an interest in zool-
ogy, not jewelry.

As wool prices reached their zenith between 1450 and 1550,
farmland was worth more as pasturage, and farm laborers were
suddenly out of work. This simple switch destroyed entire ham-
lets. It was the history of one such hamlet Billy was describing.
The topic of her dissertation turned Francis glassy-eyed: his
passion for Billy did not mitigate his indifference to the medieval wool trade. The business of money, which held no charm
for Billy at all, was Francis's meat and drink. He loved to put
together a complicated transaction. This left Billy cold. Economics was a science, an art, an *approach* to things. Francis, on
the other hand, delighted in making money. What were they
doing together? Billy wondered.

The doorbell rang. The extraordinary irritant had arrived.
He hung his dripping raincoat on a hook in the hall and surveyed Billy. She stood before him wearing a football jersey, a
pair of faded trousers, and socks.

"A vision of radiant loveliness," Francis said.

"I'm so sorry," Billy said. "The laundry ruined my filmy
peignoir."

"Get me a towel," said Francis. "I'm soaked."

He followed her upstairs to the bathroom and permitted a towel to be hung around his neck. The bathroom was at the top of the stairs. Next to it was Billy's study, where, on Billy's hard, ratty couch, she and Francis had been lovers many times. Francis was tall and slender. His hair was turning gray on the sides. He looked down at Billy and she looked up at him. In an instant they were in each other's arms and very soon thereafter they found themselves on Billy's couch. Meanwhile, a thunderstorm moved overhead, accompanied by dangerous lightning as Francis and Billy lay on Billy's couch covered by the limp, faded quilt.

"You look happy," Billy said.

"Of course I look happy," said Francis. "Aren't you happy?"

He was answered by one of Billy's long silences.

"Aren't you?" he said again.

"No."

"You're never happy with me?"

"No," said Billy.

Francis sat up. The quilt slipped off his somewhat bony shoulder. He turned to her.

"Is that true?" he said.

"Yes," said Billy. "That doesn't mean I don't want to be with you. It just means that I'm not very happy about these circumstances. It doesn't seem very appropriate to be happy."

This time Francis was silent.

"I'm starving," he said after a while.

"Umm," said Billy. She had drifted away. Outside the rain beat down and the thunder was so loud it made the windows rattle.

"Really starving," Francis said. "I don't suppose you have as much as a moldy piece of bread in your so-called pantry."

"Not so much as," said Billy, yawning. Francis could count on the fingers of one hand the meals she had given him, mostly canned soup.

"Let's go to my house," Francis said.

"Never," said Billy, who was phobic about Francis's dwelling.

"It's too rainy to go looking for a restaurant," Francis said. "I have some choice edibles at my place."

"I would rather eat cheese and garlic and live in a windmill," said Billy.

"Oh, really?" Francis said. "Where'd you pick that up?"

"It's from *Henry the Fourth*," Billy said. "My favorite teacher, Miss Chaffee, used to say it all the time."

"Cheese and garlic," Francis said. "How I long for it. Get dressed. You've given me a ferocious appetite."

Billy yawned again. She was starving, too. Hunger made Francis restless. In his naked state he prowled around her study. He knew in advance that there was nothing of interest on her desk, so he opened her study closet, where her clothes were kept.

"I always hope I'll find something nice-looking in here."

"Fat chance," said Billy.

Francis surveyed her clothes. He rummaged in the back and pulled forth a blue cotton dress.

"What's this?" he said. "This is an actual nice-looking garment."

"It was at the cleaners for a year," Billy said. "I found the ticket by accident and picked it up the other day." She turned on her side because she did not want to look at Francis. The sight of him naked and holding up her dress caused her heart to ache. These poignant moments, of which there seemed so many in a love affair, printed themselves indelibly on her consciousness. The result was that even on the happiest day, walking across a field in Maine out on a bird walk with Grey, for instance, these tender specters—Francis doing some preposterous thing—rose up before her and reminded her that her life was full of thorns.

Francis put on his trousers and socks and sat down next to

her on the couch. At his feet lay the white cotton underpants he was given to understand she bought at the five-and-ten-cent store. Next to Grey's football jersey, coiled like worms, were two worm-colored socks. The look on Francis's face said: "Why are so many of her clothes *worm*-colored?" Billy knew this look very well.

"I'll take you to my house and feed you a beautiful roast beef sandwich with watercress and curried mayonnaise," Francis said into her hair.

"I'm not going to eat the leftovers of your dinner party," Billy said.

"It wasn't a dinner party," Francis said into her neck. "It was family dinner right before Vera left."

"Eeep!" said Billy, pulling away from him. "How can you utter the word 'family' and slobber over me at the same time? Quentin and Aaron are probably coming out in hives right now and don't know why." Quentin and Aaron were Francis's grown sons.

"Hush," said Francis.

"You want to feed me *old* food," Billy said. "You want to feed me something cooked by your very own wife."

"Hush," said Francis again. He put his arms around her.

"You have very long arms," Billy said. "Has this been pointed out to you?"

"Many times," Francis said. "You have pointed it out on many occasions." He turned her toward him and kissed her.

"You have the wingspan of the California condor," Billy said.

"The California condor is extinct," Francis murmured.

"It is not," said Billy. "It is almost extinct but is making a comeback." She draped her arms around Francis's neck. "In fact," she continued dreamily, "the last issue of *Condor Watch* describes how to feed condor hatchlings on simulated vulture regurgitation."

"Sounds good to me," said Francis. "Get up."

In the kitchen they made a snack of peanut butter and stale water crackers. They were both ravenous and almost anything would have done.

Billy and Francis never stayed together—Billy sent him out into the rain and off to sleep alone. She did not like Francis prowling around her bedroom, which he did every chance he got. Francis was a terrible snoop. Accused of this, he claimed he would never go through her mail if she ever *told* him anything. Left alone he would doubtless have gone through all her bureau drawers, too.

After Francis left, Billy washed the teacups, locked the door, and checked the windows. Then she went upstairs and got into bed.

The bedroom Billy shared with Grey was the nicest room in the house. Billy and Grey were mostly indifferent to objects, and their idea of home decor had to do with placing inherited possessions here and there. In the bedroom, this inheritance was not only harmonious, it was actually pretty, a fact Billy had seen register on Francis's face.

Billy sat up. In the corner was the oak valet that for years had stood by her grandfather's closet. Now it was Grey's and when he was home his jacket hung on its shoulders, his trousers over its rack, and his watch and cuff links sat in its little tray. When he was not home it was as bare as a skeleton.

Billy had known Grey all her life. Both their fathers had worked in London, and at the same day school favored by American parents, Billy and Grey had met. Billy could easily remember him: a sturdy, wavy-haired boy wearing gray shorts, gray knee socks, and a football jersey, his fogged-up glasses concealing a fierce air of concentration. Both of them had been sent to college in America, and they had re-met in London when Billy was in graduate school and Grey was finishing at the London School of Economics.

In matters of the heart, Grey was rather a cave boy. He had hit Billy over the head, so to speak, and carried her off to his den. It had been their almost immediate intention to marry: they were both the sort who cannot imagine marrying someone they have not known forever.

Thus Billy had been a love object and a marriage object but she had never, so far as she knew, ever been the inspiration for anyone's romantic fantasy. The love affairs she had had in college with serious boys who liked to read were more like study dates than romantic encounters.

On Grey's side of the bed were his pile of astronomy books, his natural history magazines, his Russian grammar. Things had their place—the water jug on Billy's side because she got thirsty at night, the hooks on the back of the door for her night shirt and Grey's pajamas. In the known world her life had order, precedent. Anything could be dragged out into the light of day to be examined.

In the unknown world was Francis, to whom she would never be legitimately connected. She could never walk out in the sunshine with him—not in any place where they might be spotted. The experience of him was educational in a way Billy had not anticipated. She did not want to have these feelings: she had been so much happier when she had been unaware she had them. They reduced the world to a kind of love comic, or something in *One Hundred Standard Plots*. These feelings led nowhere. Unfortunately, they were hard to give up, although they caused pain more often than not. She rolled over to Grey's side of the bed, put her arms around his pillow, and fell asleep.

The next morning Francis turned up before noon. He knew Grey's schedule by heart—those parts of it Billy revealed to him. He knew when Grey was away, and if Vera was away too, as happened infrequently, he took advantage of this felicitous circumstance by seeing Billy as much as possible.

"I came for elevenses," he said.

"Oh, dear," said Billy. "There isn't anything for elevenses." A nicer mistress, she had been told, would have kept a little something or other around to feed a person.

"I'll just have you for elevenses," Francis said. Billy's heart seemed to slip. It never ceased to amaze her that the only thing she had to offer—herself—was what Francis seemed to want.

"I'm sure you'd rather have a lovely sandwich," Billy said.

"You'll do quite well," Francis said. "After all, I can always have a lovely sandwich. We can have lunch out later."

They went for lunch to one of their haunts—a seedy delicatessen in an out-of-the-way neighborhood.

Billy wolfed down her pastrami sandwich and was watching Francis, a slow eater, slowly finish his matzoh ball soup. She leaned over and took a nip with her spoon.

"Get your own soup," said Francis.

"I'm much happier with yours," Billy said. "Or don't you like to have people eat off your plate?"

"You're the only person who does," said Francis. "I rather do like it."

Billy stared at him. Married all these years and Vera never snagged so much as a chicken wing?

"Really?" she said. "Then you won't mind if I take a sip of your iced coffee."

"Vera feels very strongly about sharing drinks," Francis said offhandedly.

"Gosh," said Billy, who knew a cue when she heard one. "Think how strongly she'd feel about sharing *you*."

Francis stared into his soup.

"On the other hand," said Billy, crunching a piece of ice, "maybe she wouldn't. Maybe she'd be relieved, or maybe she would think of it as another opportunity for good works. Maybe she'd say: Oh, that poorly dressed Billy Delielle. Surely she deserved a crack at Francis to dress her up a little."

Francis did not respond. It was Billy's theory that she had been given the function in Francis's life of hating Vera.

Billy was sick of Vera. She was sick of hearing about the library for handicapped citizens which Vera was designing free of charge. A million do-good projects did not compensate for the fact that Vera had strong feelings about sharing drinks.

She felt she knew Vera like the back of her hand. She knew the names of Vera's three closest friends as well as the names of their husbands, children, and pets. She knew the history of Vera's career as an interior designer. She had heard three or four or five times the story of how Vera had packed an entire set of yellow French crockery into her suitcase by seamailing all her clothes home from Paris. She had had replayed conversations between Vera and someone called Dr. Holleys Wiener, a director of the soon-to-be-built Rees-DeGroot Library for Handicapped Citizens, conversations revealing that Vera had discovered design angles to help the handicapped that even he, Dr. Holleys Wiener, an expert in the field, had never imagined.

She had, of course, met Vera. Soon after Billy and Francis had been introduced, Francis thought it a jolly idea to invite his new friend and his new friend's husband for dinner. The yellow crockery, Billy recalled, had been much in evidence. Since she had already been told the yellow crockery story at least once, she spent a good deal of the dinner party wondering how Vera had gotten all those plates, cups, saucers, and bowls, to say nothing of an oversized platter and a number of serving pieces, into a suitcase.

Vera had been wearing a black dress with bat sleeves, black

stockings, black high-heeled sandals, and a necklace of African amber. She was wiry, lean and chic, and wore her chestnut-colored hair piled on top of her head in a stylish knot. She had small, strong, efficient-looking hands, and Billy had already been told a number of times that Vera was an ace cook who had been trained at a cooking school in France.

In the dining room, next to the carving knife and fork and the oversized yellow platter, Billy had noticed two hat pins, one topped with amber and one with coral. She could not imagine what hat pins were doing on a sideboard, but she found out.

Dinner was glazed duck, and while Francis attended to the wine, Vera prepared to carve. She rolled up her bat sleeves and stuck a hat pin in each one to keep it from unrolling while she sliced. Whenever the thought of Vera kept Billy up at night, she usually appeared in her black dress about to carve the ducks with the hat pins through her sleeves.

And now she was sitting in a crummy delicatessen with Vera's husband, who was reading the paper and checking out the local movies.

"I think we should see *It Oozed from Mars* and *Ghost Dogs from Outer Space*," Francis said. "They're playing right around the corner."

Billy knew that Vera, who liked a film with high social or artistic content, would never go to see any such film. At the same time she felt a combination of longing and despair because *Ghost Dogs from Outer Space* was just the sort of movie Grey liked to see, although Billy would never have told Francis so.

Billy never told Francis anything about Grey. Every now and again he said: "You never talk about Grey." If Billy told him something—that Grey knew how to play fives, that Grey had been taught to knit as a child, that Grey knew Russian and read about astronomy—a terrible blank look came over Francis's features and Billy would say: "You asked."

She did not know which was worse—the huge bundle of information she was constantly given about Vera, or to get no information at all. Of course, the things they really wanted to know were unaskable.

Billy fell asleep in *Ghost Dogs from Outer Space* but woke up just in time to see an asteroid destroy the entire canine ghost fleet. She was hungry and she said so.

"You have the metabolism of a child," Francis said. "You're either hungry or sleepy. In between, you're cranky."

"Little children don't have complications in their emotional lives that tire them out," said Billy.

"Oh," said Francis. "Am I a complication?" He seemed thrilled with the idea.

Just as they had a lunch haunt, so did they have a dinner spot—a Chinese restaurant in which they had never seen another Occidental. It was not a very pretty place. It had tile walls, worn linoleum on the floor, and the menus were soft with age. Taped to the wall, on shirt cardboards, were the specials of the day, written in Chinese. Billy and Francis always had the same meal: flat noodles with meat sauce, steamed broccoli, and fried fish. As they began to eat, it began to rain so dramatically that it was impossible to see across the street.

"Did you ever notice how often we're together in extreme weather?" Francis observed.

It was true. They had kept company during the two worst blizzards in fifty years, through the hottest December on record, the coldest June, the rainiest October, and they had seen snow squalls in April and had once broken up on a day when a tornado watch had been in effect.

"Just think," Billy said, "if someone says to you 'Remember the ice storm of two years ago?' you will be forced to remember that you spent it messing around with me."

Francis did not say, as he often did: "I wish you wouldn't use the term 'messing around.'" He stared out the window and remarked that the rain seemed to be letting up.

Of course it was hard to know what other people remembered. Did Billy remember each blizzard, each drought, each heat wave by Francis's presence during it? That was the thing about a love affair. It went by frame by frame, unlike ordinary life, which unrolled slowly and surely, whose high moments did not tear your heart apart when you thought of them because they were affixed, as surely as a turquoise in a silver bracelet, in context. The time Billy and Francis spent together had a beginning and an end. The middle was full of moments, of one sort or another. It was like a movie—it was like a French movie, Francis said, in which the lovers leave a Chinese restaurant, as they did now, when they thought a rainstorm had let up, only to find themselves pressed together in the doorway of an Oriental grocery store, penned in by what looked like a monsoon. Francis could see the raindrops on Billy's face, and he would see them many times again, just as he frequently conjured her up putting on her shabby clothes or standing under a ginkgo tree in autumn and letting the yellow, fan-shaped leaves drift past her shoulders.

Billy was half asleep in the car on the way home. Love was full of shadows. Even a child of three knew that the illicit lover and his wife were stand-ins for the mother and father. She looked over groggily at Francis. He did not remind her of her father. She yawned and squirmed. She longed to be home alone in her rightful bed with her head pressed against Grey's pillow and to go to sleep as if she were innocent again and the way before her was straight as a shot arrow.

Grey was due back Friday afternoon, and Vera on Saturday at noon. On Thursday morning the sky cleared and after a week

of clouds and rain, the sun came out. Francis appeared at Billy's
door with a bouquet of flowers in green florist's tissue.

"It's too beautiful to stay indoors," he said.

"Is 'stay indoors' a euphemism for going upstairs and have
you throw yourself at me?"

"We're going for a walk," said Francis. "In your closet is a
yellow dress with short sleeves. I'll pay you to take off those re-
pellent trousers and put that dress on."

Billy went upstairs obediently and changed her clothes. She
knew from past experience that Francis had a reluctance, like
Vera's about sharing drinks, about sharing Billy the day his wife
was about to return home. These niceties made less difference to
Billy, who lived with her conflicted feelings as if they had been
a broken leg.

When she got downstairs, Francis was reading her mail—he
did this every chance he got.

"The Medieval Society," he said, holding up a pamphlet. "The
telephone bill. Why don't you ever get any interesting mail?
What's this?" He picked up an air letter, clearly from Grey,
which Billy plucked from his fingers.

"This is my interesting mail," she said. "Let's go."

They drove to an out-of-the-way park they had discovered quite
early in their love affair.

"What an entertainment you are," said Francis as Billy
yawned next to him. Billy was exhausted. She had been with
Francis every day and it made her feel as if she had been living
in the weird atmosphere of another planet—like a ghost dog
from outer space. Gesture, nuance, feeling, poignancy—how
draining these things were!

The air in the park was perfectly still. The sun poured down.

"Maybe we should knock it off for a while," said Billy as they
walked to the park gate.

"A first," Francis said. "A breakup in nice weather. Do you remember the first time we came here?"

Billy remembered. It had been winter and the park lay under snow. The cardinals, starlings, and blue jays called from the bare trees. The great, gnarled mulberry tree had been gray and empty. The following June, Francis and Billy had taken a sunbath near it and watched two Slavic ladies gathering ripe mulberries into a basket.

Now the park was in its early blossom, blooming with pink and orange azalea. The dogwood and magnolia were out, and the path was scattered with petals. The scotch broom was covered with little waxy yellow flowers.

They walked without speaking, each thinking a million things. Real life opened before them: their spouses home in their rightful places. In July and August, the Clemenses went to a house in the South of France. In August, Billy and Grey went to Maine.

The next time Billy and Francis came to this park—although they might part for good and never come back—the leaves would have turned from green to red and yellow. The cedar waxwings would be eating the last of the crab apples. The light would have turned from gold to silver and the air would be chill.

But now the sunshine warmed them. They walked with their arms entwined. Francis kissed the top of Billy's hair, which was warm and sweet.

A few violets bloomed beneath a birch tree. Francis picked one and stuck it behind Billy's ear. Billy picked a spray of broom and put it through Francis's buttonhole.

Thus bedecked, they ambled. Actually they were killing time and putting a spin on their last moments all at once. They might part forever—it hardly mattered. These moments, so vivid and intense, were as enduring and specific as a piece of music, and could be replayed over and over again.

As they walked through a grove of poplar trees, the light

speckled their arms. Above them cardinals, starlings, and chick- adees called to one another. The lawn was dotted with dande- lions and buttercups. This pleasant afternoon might be tempo- rarily forgotten, but with the merest effort surely it could be called back in almost perfect detail.

A Little Something

Late one Saturday afternoon at the beginning of the new year, Francis Clemens sat at a dining room table waiting for his soup to cool. In his own household, the food was generally excellent, but he was not in his own household and the soup he was about to eat had come straight from a can. It was accompanied by two sad-looking pieces of toast that had the texture and taste of corkboard. The butter on this bread tasted, as his wife, Vera, would have said, "a little iceboxy."

Francis wore twill trousers, a blue shirt, and a pair of socks. His shoes and underwear were upstairs, and his wife was in Hawaii redesigning the house of a famous dancer.

Across from Francis, nibbling a saltine, was Billy Delielle. As usual, she was sleepy. She dipped the end of her saltine into her soup and licked it absently. She looked like a baby learning to eat.

"What a sight you are," said Francis tenderly. She was not quite awake.

"You look rather sweet," she said. "You look like a ruined satyr. Your hair is all mussed."

Francis patted his hair into place. "When we finish this awful soup, let's go upstairs and take a nap."

"Nap," snorted Billy. "That'll be the day."

She was wearing his sweater which made Francis's heart flutter. He could never quite get over her, even if he had just seen her three seconds before. He peered to see if she was going to finish her soup. He was starving and he knew he had eaten the last of the bread. He reflected that he never got enough to eat at Billy's and that, no matter how much he got of her, his hunger for her never quite abated. He looked out the window to see that it was sleeting. The idea of going out into the cold to get a decent lunch held little charm. Under the table he nudged her with his foot.

"Hey," he said.

Billy looked up. She was half asleep. "Hey what?" she said.

"I'm starving."

"Hmm," said Billy.

"I require an egg," said Francis. "More soup. Anything."

"There aren't any eggs," Billy said. "I ate the last one."

"Soup," said Francis.

"There isn't any more," said Billy. "This is the last can."

"A saltine."

"This is the last saltine," said Billy. "Do you want half of it?"

Francis regarded the saltine half. It looked wet and it was not, in fact, half. It was more a scant third.

"There's some wheat germ," said Billie. "On second thought, there's not. Gee, I'm not good for much, am I?"

"Not for food," said Francis. "But you have compensating charms."

"Hey," said Billy. "I know what. You stay here."

She went into the kitchen and returned carrying a pottery
terrine in the shape of a goose. Francis knew at once that it was
full of pâté de foie gras.

"I forgot about this," Billy said. "Grey's uncle sent it to us
ages ago. And look! Water biscuits."

Francis adored foie gras. He thought, longingly, of brown bread
with Normandy butter, endive salad, chilled white wine, and
spicy little *cornichons* to go with it, but here at Billy's table,
they ate their slices on stale water biscuits. He thought of other
meals he would like to have with it: double consommé with
tiny meat dumplings, Bibb lettuce with mustard dressing, toast
points. On white plates with big linen napkins. This was his
way of making mental reference to Vera, who knew how to
serve foie gras, without thinking about her.

Francis considered himself an excellent husband. He fetched
his wife's luggage, picked her up from the airport and carried
her thence, drew her bath when she was tired, weather-stripped
the bedroom windows, saw to her investments, gave financial
advice to members of her family, was moderate in his habits
and, in general, was a cheering sort of companion. His many
years with Vera were rich in history.

And yet, he thought, as he gazed at the top of Billy's head,
at his age a man required a little light and dark—a little something that made the images of life as clear and startling as those
on a photographic plate.

Francis often thought of this love affair in architectural terms
—as a folly or gazebo or some small chapel done in California
Spanish Gothic. Whatever it was, it was an eccentric structure
full of twists, turns, gargoyles, and mazes—a kind of created
wilderness, like the gardens of Capability Brown.

He smiled across the table. A smile stole—the only way it ever got there—across Billy's features. It quite lit up her face and reminded Francis how much he loved her.

"It's so rare to see you smile," he said with a catch in his voice. "Each time I see it, I always think I ought to have a picture of it."

"Smart idea," said Billy. "You could make it into postcards and send it to your friends at Christmas."

Late at night Francis went out into the cold and drove to his own abode to sleep alone. He and Billy did not have what Billy referred to as "sleep-over dates." The ostensible reason for the shunning of sleep-over dates was the late-night telephone call from a traveling spouse, but the truth, although Francis was not sure quite *what* the truth was, was probably more complicated. For instance, Billy hated his house and usually refused to set a foot within it. Therefore their dealings took place at Billy's. Furthermore, she became extremely uneasy whenever Francis followed her into her bedroom. Francis, of course, followed her any chance he got—when she went to change her clothes, for example. He had noticed with an unpleasant jolt that the bed his mistress shared with her husband was rather small, whereas the bed he shared with his wife was rather large.

Late at night it was not unusual for Francis to find himself wide awake, exhausted, and unable to sleep. The theme of this insomnia was Grey Delielle. Often he simply held an image of Grey in his mind—Grey with his elbows on Francis's dinner table talking in his soft, intelligent voice, an image from the one dinner party Billy and Grey had been to, although they had been invited several times.

What did he know about Grey? That he had done graduate work at the London School of Economics and had worked on Wall Street for a year before he quit in a combination of boredom and despondency. He had been snapped up to be economic adviser and troubleshooter at the Valeur Foundation, where he wrote white papers on economic trends and represented the foundation at various seminars and policy meetings here and abroad. He had invented the Delielle curve, which predicted the fluctuation of interest rates. He had two sisters, Helena and Alice. Helena, Francis seemed to remember, lived with her husband and children in Scotland. He could not remember what Alice did. Perhaps Billy had never said. Grey had studied Russian and as an undergraduate had had a fellowship for a year at the University of Leningrad. He was a minor expert on iron curtain country economies.

He was five feet eleven and a half, had wavy brown hair, and wore the kind of glasses the National Health gives out—plain, round, with a wire rim. He liked racket sports—had Francis once entertained the notion of playing squash with him?—and also loved soccer.

The only subject on which Billy was forthcoming about Grey was his relationship to the natural world: he was a trout fisherman, a tier of flies, a finder and cataloger of bird's nests, fossils, animal bones. He was interested in flora and fauna of all kinds, in contrast to Francis, who liked cut flowers and domestic animals such as Irish terriers and beef cows.

And what did this amount to? Billy's real life was Grey. They almost looked alike: well made, dark-haired, solid.

These reflections made his heart pound.

Every once in a while he would try to snag another crumb of information from his beloved.

"About you and Grey," he would begin. A perfectly blank look would cover Billy's features. She did not approve of this sort of conversation. Francis had to admit that she had never solicited anything about Vera: he had always told her more than she ever wanted to know.

"Why not discuss it?" Francis said.

Billy gave him a long look and said it was a moral issue.

"I don't see this as a moral issue," Francis said.

"How fascinating," said Billy. "You don't see adultery as a moral issue."

"No, I don't," Francis said defensively. "This is the twentieth century. We are two grown people who are hurting no one at all. We are sincerely fond of one another. I think what we are doing is entirely on the up-and-up. And besides, if it *is* immoral, you don't have much right getting sticky on smaller points like not talking about your husband."

When Francis looked at Billy he saw an expression on her face he had never seen before, of awful sadness and tension. It made him realize that she *did* see this as a moral issue. How far apart they were!

"Do you feel you're doing something wrong?" said Francis in the fatherly tone he could not prevent and which she hated.

"Obviously."

"So why do you do it?"

"Obviously I can't triumph over my immoral side," said Billy, and that was the end of that conversation.

Francis had actually been shocked. How hopeless it seemed ever to know another person!

Often he asked Billy if he might stay over and sleep with her in her bed just to see what she would say. He felt he was entitled to this barometer of her feeling.

He asked as he was putting on his coat.

"Why don't we go over to your house and sleep in *your* bed?" she said, as she often did.

Francis, of course, did not answer because he did not ever want Billy to know what great appeal this idea had for him. As he drove home slowly in the snow he wondered how he was going to account for his time when Vera called, if, in fact, she had called during the day. He made up a double feature of outer-space horror movies—*Avengers from Planet X* and *Shards of*

Death. Francis often went to what Vera thought were idiotic films, but he considered them material and often used them in his columns.

But Vera had not called all day, and when she did call, she was tired and Francis was tired and therefore he did not get to use his invented movies. This depressed him. Even more depressing was the icy coldness of the sheets as he slipped into bed. He lay half frozen and then, in a fit of longing, he dialed Billy's number. Her line was busy.

In his tired, cold state, sleep eluded him. Instead of sinking back into gentle slumber, he found himself as usual possessed of a fixed idea: Grey Delielle and how little he knew about him. He had snooped in Grey's closet—a row of charcoal and blue business suits, a pair of binoculars on a hook, a chart of the heavens tacked to the door, a pair of hiking boots. Next to his bed was a pile of mysteries and two astronomy books. He wore a flannel robe. His handwriting was minuscule and looked, from a little distance, like tiny insect droppings. Francis knew this because he had tried to read various notes of Grey's on Billy's desk. That tiny script disturbed Francis. What sort of person was it who made his handwriting so purposefully minimal and yet expected to be read? Was it a form of arrogance? Was this person capable of writing a love letter? Did whatever lay behind this insectlike handwriting have anything to contribute to whatever reasons Billy had for conducting a secret love affair? Billy and Grey were as mysterious as creatures from Planet X. He knew that Billy and Grey had both grown up in London and known each other in childhood. Did this mean they were bored with each other, or incredibly close? With these unpleasant and unanswerable questions flopping around in his head like a bat that had mistakenly flown in through the living room window, Francis fell asleep.

. . .

The next morning he jumped into his clothes, called Billy and woke her up, and dashed into the kitchen for a quick cup of tea. His eye fell on the Clemenses' old picnic basket, which was kept on top of the sideboard. He got it down and filled it with a box of good tea, a tin of kippers, a half-dozen eggs, a package of oatcakes, a loaf of homemade whole wheat bread, which had been kept in the freezer, and a stick of butter. With this load he trudged into the blowing snow, well aware of what a picture he made. Only a man very far gone in some way would make such a preposterous gesture.

On the stairs of her house he saw that the Sunday paper had been delivered. As he scooped it up in his arms he realized how *other* the life of the other is. He had no idea that the Delielles got their Sunday paper delivered. He looked around him. There was not a soul on the street. He stood at Billy's door with his picnic basket in his hand.

"Well, well. Father Christmas," said Billy when she opened the door.

Francis shook himself, took off his boots, and hung his coat and hat on the Delielles' hat rack. Billy was wearing exactly what she had been wearing yesterday and would wear tomorrow. She had not yet brushed her hair, which was mussed on one side and flat on the other, and there was a fleck of toothpaste on her upper lip. His heart expanded like a bellows, and he took her into his arms.

"No hanky-panky before breakfast," said Billy. "I hope there's something to eat in there."

This hurt Francis's feelings. If she could not put on something less hideous to greet him in, at least she might spare him a crumb, but when he entered the kitchen, he saw she had not been idle. She too had been out and had provisioned eggs, English muffins, strawberry jam, and five cans of split pea soup.

They watched the snow fall as they had their breakfast, and then they went upstairs to Billy's study and bedded down on her awful couch, giving Francis a chance to reflect, as he had reflected many times before, what a bare and ugly setting this was for love.

Then it was time for lunch. By this time the snow had stopped and Francis suggested a walk.

"Too cold," Billy said.

"I'm restless," Francis said. "Come home with me and we'll hang around my house for a change."

"Never," said Billy.

"It isn't fair," Francis said. Billy looked at him.

"I don't have to be fair," she said. "Besides, the little buggers are always dropping by."

"I wish you wouldn't refer to my sons as the little buggers," Francis said.

"You're absolutely right," said Billy. "They're grown-up buggers now."

"They won't drop in," Francis said. "They're off skiing with their sweethearts."

"What about Miss Thompson?" said Billy, referring to Francis's upstairs tenant.

"In England."

"And the little Sutcliffes?"

"The little Sutcliffes never leave their snug little bunk except to go to work. They're probably all curled up under a fuzzy blanket with their Angora cat."

"I still don't want to go."

"Nonsense, girl. Into your snowsuit."

Francis's hallway was papered in dark green, with a design of red and yellow medallions. The floor was polished wood and had an old Persian runner on it. The hall table had been sent back from France and held a large faïence bowl—also brought back from France—in which keys and change and ticket stubs and mail were kept. The hall chair—an English chair carved from a single log—had been a present from Francis to Vera. Billy sat in it, taking off her boots.

Francis asked her to hurry—she had been taking off her boots for several hours, he felt. She looked up at him. Her hair fell into her eyes. "I hate it here," she said.

It made Francis glow that she hated his dwelling. No one but a person in love with him could have hated it.

He led her into the kitchen, a room Francis particularly loved. It had the original beams, a fireplace, a well-stocked pantry, and a large, old Welsh cupboard on whose shelves were stacked Vera's collection of yellow crockery. The kitchen table had been made by Swedish peasants. Billy sat down at the table. Francis made her a cup of tea.

"Don't you feel awfully exposed with all this stuff around?" she said.

"Do you mean afraid of being burgled?"

"I mean, out in the open," Billy said. "All your taste is on display. People assume what you're like before they hardly get into the living room."

No one in the world, Francis thought, could ever have told much about Billy by looking at her. She had little to display. The vital things about her were willfully hidden. He watched her drink her cup of tea out of one of the yellow cups. He wished he could freeze the moment and have her forever sitting at the kitchen table with the light casting a sheen on her lank hair, with her sleeves rolled up to reveal her flat forearms.

"What would Grey say if he found out about us?" Francis suddenly said.

"He would be very disappointed," Billy said. "He thinks I'm honorable."

"And seeing me means you aren't?"

"Grey's a very serious person," Billy said.

The implication that Francis was not a very serious person hung in the air, and Billy did nothing to dispel it.

"Vera's pretty sophisticated," said Francis. "She'd be mad, but I don't think she'd disapprove."

"In that case," said Billy, "I'll just leave her a little note."

When Francis finished his tea he realized how tired he was. He was in his own house and he craved sleep. He looked at Billy. The expression on her face told him how ardently she wished she were at home.

"Let's take a nap," he said. "A real one." He took her gently by the elbow. "I'm falling down. Come and curl up next to me."

He led her down the hallway toward the bedroom, and he could feel the reluctance in her step. It was like walking in a dream: so familiar, so out of context. The walls of the bedroom were butter yellow and on the bed was the huge blue and white coverlet Vera had commissioned, a reproduction of an early American design called Lonesome Pine Tree.

Suddenly Billy bolted. "Not here," she said.

Of course Francis had known all along that Billy was not going to lie down with him in his own bedroom. He knew that if they were to lie down at all it would be in the guest room, which was very drafty. Francis loved these demonstrations of Billy's reluctance. Since such intense resistance did not prevent her from being with him, was that not a declaration of love?

As they walked down the hall Francis felt his throat go hot. It might have been ferocious sadness, or he might be getting the flu. If he did get the flu he would give it to Billy—a truly shared experience.

In his bones he knew that this was the last time Billy would ever wander around his house and he wanted her there. He felt he was laying in a store of memories almost as you stock a pantry with emergency supplies.

The guest room was cold. In the snow, the light from the

window was milky blue. There was not a sound except the sounds houses make when they seem to breathe. Francis felt he could not bear the depths of his feelings in the silent room.

"Jesus, it's freezing," he said. "Hop under this quilt and warm me up."

It was Billy who fell asleep at once. Francis closed his eyes. His bones hurt. This afternoon would be as if etched in glass: bright, hard, and clear. It was his to have: he could conjure it up whenever he wanted, wherever he was.

Billy stirred in his arms. Francis stirred, too. He was half asleep and he was thirsty, but he was too tired to know just what it was he was thirsty for.

Swan Song

Just before Thanksgiving, during a freak hot spell, Francis Clemens and Billy Delielle decided to part. They had come to this conclusion many times before—Billy was usually the instigator. She had tried to break up a number of times. Being married and having a love affair made her frantic, although she often got the sense from Francis that he had been married for so long it hardly counted.

Billy was glum and cranky. In this sultry weather, she was crankier than usual. She pushed her lank brown hair off her face with an exasperated gesture Francis had seen thousands of times.

"I think we ought to have a serious talk," Billy said. "I mean, what passes for serious talk between you and me."

Francis, who had been standing in her stuffy kitchen for half an hour, was braced.

"*I* feel we talk on a very high level," he said. "But of course you mean you think we ought to break up."

"Breaking up is what teenagers do," Billy said.

"And as adults we should find some more mature and noble method," said Francis.

"Yes," said Billy, who managed not to look at Francis but at her toaster. "This can't be doing anyone any good. I don't like sneaking around with you or waiting until our mates are away. Besides, you take up all my time blathering on the telephone."

"I don't notice you hanging up in protest, miss," Francis said.

"I have reservoirs of kindness about which you know nothing," Billy said. She gave him the merest grin, a sort of twist of her downy upper lip.

"Well, then," Francis said. "You're quite definite?"

"Quite," said Billy.

"All right," said Francis, in a not uncheerful voice. He liked to take these breakups seriously, but they never lasted very long and made him feel that at least he had made some sort of effort. "If we *are* going to break up, let's go upstairs and say good-bye properly."

"You mean you want to go upstairs to my study so you can hurl yourself at me," said Billy.

"I wish you could put it more delicately," Francis said. "Throw, for instance, or pitch. Let's go."

"I think it's a pretty stupid idea," said Billy.

"Is that going to stand in your way?" Francis said.

"Obviously not," said Billy, with a sigh.

Francis had an affection for Billy's study, since many of life's sweet moments had been passed on her nasty little couch. How often he had looked around him, to the plain office desk, the gray metal shelves, the white filing cabinets, and wondered about the woman in his arms. At these moments she was in some way more alien than ever. He pressed her head against him. Her hair smelled of wheat biscuits. Francis looked at her lovingly.

"About our little chat," she said.

"All right," said Francis. "Let's get out of here and go for a walk."

They drove in Francis's car to a quiet park far from their households. When they were not breaking up, they might walk with their arms around each other, or kiss by the stone wall. On the way they did not discuss their future. Instead, they discussed the coming holiday.

"And you're going to that cousin of Grey's—what's-her-name —Vanessa?—in Boston?" Francis said. His voice had the formal paternal tone he used when referring to Billy and her lawful wedded husband.

"Yup," said Billy. She knew this was her cue. "And you all," she said chirpily, "are staying here."

"Yes," said Francis, with relief. "Quentin is bringing his girl friend and Aaron is bringing his college classmate Joe and Joe's little sister Amy. Their family is all scattered."

Billy, who was used to hearing descriptions of Clemens family gatherings, said, "Oh, poor little Joe and Amy. Little waifs and strays. How lucky they are to have the bosom of your family to nestle in."

Francis did not respond.

"Oh, cheer up, Frank," said Billy. "Tell me who else is coming."

This actually did cheer Francis. It made him feel for a moment that he had a fighting chance to have a simple life—one in which people had family Thanksgivings and no love affairs. Billy did not think that family was a fit subject for lovers, but to Francis it was as necessary as oxygen to a fire.

"Never mind," said Billy. "I'll tell you all about Vanessa and her husband, Arthur. Their children are called Leda, Amos, Ben, and Matilda, and two of them have broken arms. Now, isn't that thrilling?"

Francis was only half listening. He could never get Billy to realize how hard it was to concentrate on conversation while looking for a place to park.

"Thrilling," he repeated.

What a terrible time of year! During the holidays a heavy fire screen of family was thrown in front of passion. The park opened before them. As they walked down the broad, central path the ground was thick with yellow leaves and the unnaturally hot weather caused tiny beads of moisture to gather on the pine branches. The sky was the color of chrome.

Francis led Billy down a lane. He had no plan in mind. When they came to the low stone wall, Francis put his arms around his mistress and kissed her. He could not deny that kissing her was like slaking a long thirst with cool, fresh water. He pulled her very near. Often he found himself holding her so tight that he could feel her ribs. Her cheek was moist next to his and he was happy to notice that she clutched him as fiercely as he clutched her. He always hoped that if he kissed her enough, if he held her tight enough, she would finally *reveal* something to him. Francis liked to be *told* things, and Billy's reluctance on certain points made him guess. The fact that she was as willing a participant in this love affair as he for some reason did not set his mind at rest. How much did she love him? Or miss him when they were apart? He unhooked himself from her and held her back so he could see her.

For an instant she looked dreamy and unfocused. Then she said: "Isn't it banal?"

"Isn't what banal?" said Francis.

"Us, sneaking off to this park to hug and kiss before a major holiday. Perhaps we should exchange menus and you can tell me Vera's recipe for chestnut stuffing again."

"*I* told you Vera's recipe?" Francis said.

"I'm positive *she* didn't call to tell me," said Billy. "You've recited it four or five times. I also heard it last year at Thanksgiving time."

Francis swallowed. Had they actually been seeing each other that long?

"Come on, Frank," she continued. "Be realistic. How do you feel looking up from your turkey at your swell family when you've just crawled out of bed with me?"

"I wish you wouldn't say 'crawled,' " said Francis.

"Okay," said Billy. "Hobbled. Well, how do you feel?"

"Divided," Francis finally said. This sort of conversation always gave him a headache in back of his eyes. He could never have compared his mistress to a summer day, but rather to one of those gray, overcast days in middle autumn when the angle of the light makes everything very clear. He looked at her. She did not pout or snicker. She simply looked serious. The sight of her made Francis's heart melt. Rarely did she ever look so undefended, and, when she did, Francis was reminded how deep an enterprise this was.

"I mean," Billy was saying, "I'm not going to leave Grey, and you're not going to leave Vera, and we're not going to run off to some cozy little island together."

Though this was a perfectly accurate summary of the facts of the matter, it rattled Francis nonetheless. Being in love, he often felt, was like having a bird caught in his hair.

Billy walked a little bit ahead of him. From her awful-looking clothes you could not imagine how sweetly she was made. Her faded skirt—had it once been green?—and the mouse-colored sweater that had belonged to her little brother touched him.

Francis caught up with her. "Look," he said. "Today is Monday. Thanksgiving is Thursday. Let's not see each other for the rest of the week. We won't talk on the telephone, either. We'll take a vacation from this love affair and see each other next week."

"Very convenient," said Billy. "Let's change the subject. Aren't you hungry? Let's have lunch."

They took their lunch as they often did in a neighborhood delicatessen near the park. At this hour of the afternoon, it was almost empty. On one mirrored wall was a cutout sign, laminated with silver, red, and green, that read: LET US CATER YOUR NEXT AFFAIR, which Francis never failed to read aloud.

"Huh," said Billy. "They certainly catered this one."

After lunch Francis drove her home, and that was the manner in which they broke up for the seventh or eighth or ninth time.

The following Monday found Francis and Billy hanging around in Billy's kitchen. Their little vacation had made them shy. Billy gave Francis a cup of tea with which he paced, trying to reestablish himself. He opened the refrigerator to see if there was anything to nibble on, but there was only bottled water, wheat germ, eggs, and a tin of imported oatmeal.

Francis was about to ask politely after her Thanksgiving when the telephone rang. Of course, he would never know who was on the other end. Billie had a wonderful telephone murmur —you would have had to kiss her to hear her—and she would never say who it was. While she was whispering into the phone, Francis amused himself by pawing through the Delielle mail, which was open and lying on the kitchen table.

His eye fell on a form letter. The letterhead read RICK'S REPTILE VILLAGE (FORMERLY RICK'S HERP HUT). It began:

> Hi there, fellow herp collector!
> We have moved to larger quarters here
> in Tashkent, Illinois. Our snakes, reptiles,
> and amphibians are of the highest quality.

> We ship only if the herp is feeding and we
> guarantee live delivery.

Billy hung up and turned to him. "Why don't you just ask what you want to know instead of snooping around?"

"What an interesting letter from Rick's Reptile Hut. Do you keep reptiles of which I am unaware?"

"Just you," snickered Billy. "Besides, if you're going to read my mail, you may as well get it right. It's *Rick's Reptile Village*."

Francis was actually stunned. His mistress got mail from reptile dealers. He had spent hours in her company and this fact was entirely unknown to him. She had never so much as mentioned a worm or lizard. "Well?"

"When we joined the North East Nature Conservancy we got on a lot of mailing lists," Billy said with reluctance.

"How quaint," Francis said. "I had no idea *you* were so inclined toward the natural sciences. I was led to believe that was the province of your husband."

Billy was silent.

"Is that what those notebooks were about?" Francis said. In her bare kitchen his voice seemed to echo.

"What notebooks?" Billy said defensively.

"You know very well which ones," said Francis. "The ones you wouldn't let me see last summer before you went off to Maine."

Billy was silent again. She looked as abashed as a schoolboy.

"They're my nature notebooks," she finally said.

"Indeed," said Francis fiercely.

"I make notes in them," said Billy, as if confessing to an unusual crime.

"A strange use for a notebook," said Francis. "Explain yourself further."

Billy sighed.

"Yes?" he said.

"When we're in Maine, we go bird walking," Billy said. "We go nature hiking. We go canoeing in swamps. Each summer I like to read one naturalist. Last summer I read Gilbert White. I take notes on what I read, and I like to take notes on what I see. Does it make you happy to know that?"

In fact it made Francis miserable to know that. A vision of Billy and her husband, in matching twill walking shorts with rucksacks on their backs and field glasses around their necks, rose up before him.

"How fetching you must look at your nature activities," said Francis. His voice, he found, was ever so slightly uneven in pitch. He looked at his mistress. She looked exhausted and distressed.

"You wanted to know," she said, staring at the floor.

"I did," said Francis.

"Well, now you know," she said and, turning from him, she leaned against the sink and began to cry. The sight of Billy in tears was such a rarity that it quite startled Francis. He knew by instinct that she believed that it was bad form to cry in public, and she would rather have hidden in the cellar. It was quite the wrong thing to approach her, but he could not hold himself off for very long. In his arms she was as unyielding as an ironing board.

"Are there any more things I don't know about you?" murmured Francis into her hair.

"Yes," said Billy, who pulled herself away from his now wet shirt front and immediately reclaimed her composure. "I'm married."

"That isn't funny," Francis said.

"Gee," said Billy. "I thought it was."

Imagine, Francis later thought as he sat alone in his own kitchen, getting so upset about a form letter from a snake breeder. After

all, it was only one of five million things they did not know
about one another. Marriage, of course, was as deep as a well,
as rich as the unicorn tapestries and with as many stitches and
as much detail. Married people suffered and rejoiced over and
over and over and over again. Marriage was a trench dug by
time, a straight furrow, the mighty oak that has grown year
after year after year from a tiny acorn. Lovers were, by compari-
son, little scratches in the ground.

Francis stared at the surface of his kitchen table and put his
head in his hands. His kitchen, unlike Billy's drab, industrial-
looking, functional space, reminded one that cooking is not
mere science. It was agleam with copper pots, French crockery,
baskets from New England. The table was over one hundred
years old. Thousands of days of family life were etched into its
surface. Francis's wife used those copper pots. He had spent
years at this table chatting to Vera while she put together one
of her delicious meals. At the moment she was in Chicago consulting on the renovation of something called the Talisman
Foundation, whose headquarters were being redesigned.

Francis's dinner was a ham sandwich he had bought at the
local delicatessen and a tall glass of beer. Had Vera been home,
he would have been staring at a wonderful-looking plate of
something or other.

This sandwich, Francis thought, was rather like Billy: unadornedly what it was. It was without butter or mayonnaise or
mustard, anything to dress it up. Unlike Billy it was dry and
satisfied his hunger. Sitting alone in the kitchen added gloom to
heartache as Francis thought he might take his beer and sandwich and sit before his television set if there was a football
game on. He felt he needed some distraction of a rough, traditional masculine sort.

He looked at the clock: it was seven thirty. He had left Billy
at five thirty. How heavy the hours seemed! Now he had the
long road of an evening before him, a man in his prime, a man

who had just spent a few hours on a hard lumpy couch in his mistress' study with his warm, pliant mistress in his arms, forced to sit alone with a dry ham sandwich for sustenance and a football game for company.

Francis knew he did such a good imitation of a conventional man, a solid family man who might be musing about his investments, or the achievements of his children, that a passing stranger or a close friend might have been fooled. Who would have thought that this man was prey to a fit of longing, and for a woman who was not only not his wife, but who was not tender, did not cajole or pet him, who was loath to put on as much as an earring to cheer him up!

He finished his sandwich. He did not have the heart to watch a football game. Instead, he reread the morning papers, paid some bills, and fiddled at his desk until Vera called, and then he went to bed. That night, like many other nights, Francis felt he was wrestling with demons. Here, in the same city, not even such a long walk away, under the same canopy of night, his mistress slept. How odd that such a small area contained them! How odd that ordinary life went running on around the stupendousness of their secret!

The next day Francis practically flew to her side. It was Billy's morning to teach and Francis knew at exactly what time her class broke. It was a cinch to park himself in the hallway near her classroom. He had done it many times before. He often wondered aloud if the students thought he was her husband, and Billy always said they thought she was his nurse.

They walked down the college path. A few wet leaves drifted off the trees. The air was alternately icy and warm. The sky was very low.

"I've got the car over here," Francis said. He felt a little out of breath. When they were both sitting in the car, Francis said, without thinking: "Do you ever miss me?"

"I thought we were supposed to discuss breaking up," said Billy, who was looking straight ahead.

"Later," Francis said. "Answer my question."

His mistress did not give him the benefit of a face for him to read. After a long time she said, almost into her lap: "Last summer I was walking by myself in a field, in Maine. I had just seen a black-billed cuckoo—I think it was a black-billed cuckoo—and I missed you so much it felt like a stomach pain and I sort of doubled over."

She said no more.

For lack of an adequate response, Francis started the car. It gave him something to do and filled the air around them with noise. He had no idea where they might be going, but at least he felt they might be about to go somewhere.

Billy was silent beside him. For once he was glad not to see what she was expressing or trying not to express. It was just as well that she was like the dark opaque side of a stained glass window. He felt he could not have stood to see her complicated lights and shadows. She was wearing less awful clothes than usual—her tweed teaching outfit—but she looked tired, sad, and full of dark thoughts, thoughts she was not going to share with Francis. Sometimes she brought out in him a streak of tenderness that bordered on the parental, and also on the violent. He wanted to take her in his arms and hear her bones crack.

Billy looked up. "Stop looking at me as if I were the daughter you never had," she said.

"You are nothing of the sort," sniffed Francis.

"Then perhaps it's true that you are abnormally attached to one of your sons," she said.

"I am abnormally attached to you," said Francis. "Now, what shall we do? Shall we go and have a spot of lunch?"

"Let's just go home," said Billy, referring to her dwelling. She and Francis, of course, had no home.

They sat in the car in front of the Delielle house.

"About breaking up," Billy said.

"Yes," said Francis jauntily. "Let's do."

"I can't do this any more," Billy said.

"I guess I can't either," Francis said.

"It's very unsettling," said Billy.

"It isn't making me calm and placid, either," said Francis.

Silence fell, in the manner of a guillotine.

"If you're going to give me up," Francis said, "I want a cup of tea before you send me into the cold."

"This isn't what I call cold," said Billy.

"You know exactly what I mean," Francis said.

As soon as they were in the kitchen, they faced each other with a wild look. Francis grabbed her arm.

"If we're going to part, let's at least have a swan song," he said.

"We've had enough swan songs to populate all the lakes in Maine," Billy said.

"I don't care," said Francis.

As they walked up the stairs to Billy's study, Francis's step was light with anticipation. His heart was pounding. He was no longer a husband, a father, a householder, a provider, or a friend. He felt as if he had little wings on the heels of his feet like the god Mercury. He was his elemental self—a lover.

The preliminaries were always the same. Billy closed her study door. Francis knew it was not necessary to lock it because this only happened when Grey was away. How fortunate that Grey's job involved travel! How lucky for Francis that young men worked so hard!

From the arm of her ratty couch, Billy took a quilt and unfolded it. It was made of faded blue cotton and had been washed a great number of times. She opened this no matter what the weather, a gesture of propriety that touched Francis's heart. Her study faced north and, without any lamps on, it was very dim. In this perpetual dusk they got undressed, and when undressed they lay down on their sides—they could barely fit any other way.

It was not the last time they would find themselves together, Francis knew in his heart. How could they separate when they were so connected? Francis knew these things troubled Billy. For his part he did not like to think of them at all. He did not care why they were together. He simply wanted what he had: his own specific Billy in his arms.

Francis, for a moment, was in a state of perfect happiness. He heard his beloved say: "Shove over, Frank, will you? You're crushing my arm." This sentence was as music to his ears.

He held her all the more tightly. He felt he wanted to breathe her in—her field glasses and bird books, her herp catalogs, her history, all her secrets: everything.

She nestled against him and he hoped ardently that they would part and rejoin over and over, into the future. After all, they had parted before. Surely it would not be final. They would find their way back to one another as swans are said to come back each year to the same still pool.

A Country Wedding

On a cool, misty morning in early June, Billy and Grey Delielle drove into the country, toward the town of North Wigsall, where Billy's oldest friend, Penny Stern, was going to be married from her grandmother's country house.

A band of fog hung over the Hudson River. Billy, who was beginning to feel damp under her hair, could see a red smudge in the hazy sky: when the sun broke through, it was going to be hot.

Grey drove, his cuffs carefully folded back. His suit jacket was hung from a hook in the back of the car—it was the suit he had worn to his own wedding eight years ago. Next to him, Billy sat poised as if encased in eggshells. She was not much of a dresser; her lack of interest in personal adornment was well documented among her friends. The bride-to-be had taken Billy in hand and the result was the blue-and-white-striped linen dress in which Billy felt imprisoned. Afraid to move or blink or sweat, she feared that the mere act of sitting in the car was wrinkling her in the back. She felt like a child trapped in a party dress, a feeling she could remember exactly. She slipped off her shoes and propped her feet on the dashboard, as she was sure a seat belt would ruin the front of her dress.

Grey was more used to being dressed than Billy, but he did not like it any more than she did. His closet was half full of sober-looking suits. The other half was full of walking shorts, hiking boots, old blue jeans, and waders for the trout season. He had been Billy's guide to nature, which she had previously experienced mostly through books. As a child she had read endlessly about bats, birds and frogs, and the life of swamps, but her parents were entirely urban, and no one had taken her into the outdoors until she met Grey. Together they had hiked, trekked, climbed, explored swamps, gone for owl walks, and kept life lists of birds. When the trout season opened Billy was perfectly happy to sit on a bank swatting midges and reading while Grey stood up to his hips in cold water. On their honeymoon they had gone to Dorset to search for fossils.

Billy, Grey, and Penny Stern had all grown up together in London, the children of American parents who had sent them to a slightly progressive, coeducational day school in Westminster. Billy had known Grey most of her life. He was three years her senior, and she could remember herself as a rather messy ten-year-old girl watching the thirteen-year-old Grey on the football field, or staring at him through the window of the science room. He was a very brainy and popular boy who played baseball in Hyde Park with his American friends. When she looked at him now, she could see the boy he had been, and she could not remember a time when she had not loved him.

After college they both came back to London where they finally re-met, at a party. The moment she saw him, Billy knew that she had found what she was looking for. It was not love at first sight. It had been love all these years. "We were imprinted on each other early, like ducks," Grey said. "They always love the first person close to them."

She remembered with perfect clarity how he looked: standing in a corner with an empty glass in his hand, his sleeves rolled up, his glasses slipping slightly down his nose, looking abstracted and slightly puzzled in the middle of a hot, noisy party. At the sight of him she felt her vision clarify, as if she had been living in a kind of half light. Suddenly everything seemed clear as if under a wide blue sky. Her destiny was plain before her: things made sense. She had never felt this way before, and she knew that if she didn't marry Grey she probably wouldn't marry anyone.

Billy was not a pursuer, but she grabbed Grey's sleeve. She was entitled, because they had known each other as children and had never been strangers to one another.

He turned around and she saw he *was* somewhat of a stranger —a grown man. Suddenly she was as shy as a child. For an instant she thought he didn't remember her, but he held her hand and said her name. Then they both smiled with amazing happiness, as if they had just gotten away with an entirely ingenious prank. They were married within six months.

Billy knew the road to Penny's grandmother's by heart. She had stayed there as a child and visited frequently as an adult. In fact, Grey had proposed to her near a swamp off Old Wall Lane, less than a mile from Mrs. Stern's house. Billy remembered that day clearly: not only had she been proposed to, but she had seen the great blue heron for the first time.

They turned off the highway and onto the country road. The sun had not yet dried off the dew, and the fat green leaves looked moist and velvety. When they unrolled the windows, the air smelled mild and sweet, of newly cut grass and chamomile.

Billy leaned back carefully. To be in a car with your husband, going to the wedding of your oldest friend, to visit a place you knew every corner of made life seem as correct, upright, and proper as a Quaker meeting house. The fact that her lawful wedded husband had not, for example, been the first man to set eyes on her new dress was the thorn in the rose, the termite lurking under the wooden porch steps.

Months ago Penny had taken Billy shopping, dragging her through a number of overheated, very expensive shops and department stores and sending her home with a beautiful blue-and-white-striped linen dress in a fancy box. Once at home alone, Billy climbed out of her teaching suit and back into her old clothes.

No sooner had she thrown her suit over a chair than the doorbell rang, and Francis Clemens appeared. He looked tenderly at her and remarked: "As always, a vision of radiant loveliness."

He closed the door behind him and took her into his arms. He was thirsty for her, but he found her reluctant. Instead of kissing him back, she led him to the kitchen for a cup of tea.

Their usual pattern was tea and then a trip upstairs to Billy's cheerless little study to lie in each other's arms on Billy's not very comfortable couch. But something final was in the air, and they did not go upstairs. Instead, at Billy's suggestion, they sat in the living room and drank their tea.

On the coffee table was the dress box. Francis, who knew one fancy shop from another, recognized it at once.

"Did someone leave this here by mistake?" he said.

"It's mine," Billy said. "It contains an expensive dress."

"Really," Francis said. "But that means you intend to wear it somewhere and we know what you think of social life."

"It's a poisoned well," Billy said. "This is for Penny's wedding in June. You know who I mean."

"The one with the formidable grandmother."

"The very one," Billy said. Penny's grandmother was the

only person in the world who called Billy by her given name of Josephine.

"Well," said Francis, stretching his legs. "It certainly would be nice to see you in it."

Billy sat on the edge of the couch. The idea of trying on this dress, which she would wear to the wedding of her oldest friend, who was one of Grey's oldest friends, struck her as very wrong. It was a violation of something. She attempted to explain this to Francis, who looked very dark.

"A woman absolves herself of guilt by brushing her teeth in the morning," he said.

Billy had never seen him angry before.

"Is that a quote?"

"It's a quote from some misogynist Spaniard whose name escapes me at the moment," said Francis. "I must say, I've never suspected you of being quite so sentimental. After all, we've been to bed together countless times and suddenly you get proprietary about a dress because you're going to wear it on some sacred occasion."

Billy opened the dress box and pulled out the dress. She shook it out and held it up in front of her.

Francis surveyed her without expression.

"Quite a departure from your usual garb," Francis said.

"You'll have to help me fold it back up," said Billy. "If I do it myself, I'll crease it."

"If you don't mind my saying," Francis said, "I think you'll want to hang it up. And you might think of putting it in a dress bag so your other garments don't smudge it."

"Very funny," said Billy. She draped the dress carefully over the box and put it on the dining room table. Then she came back and sat down on the sofa. Francis sat down next to her.

"This has to stop," Billy said. "My life is being ruined."

"I knew it," Francis said. "A nuptial rears its ugly head and suddenly you want to break up."

"I always want to break up."

"Is that really true?" Francis said.

"Yes," said Billy. "Isn't it true for you?"

Francis was silent. It was not, in fact, true for him. "That's a terrible thing to say," he said.

"Truth is not always lovely," quoted Billy. Francis regarded her.

"Sometimes I'd really like to pop you one," he said. He took her warm hand and they sat on the sofa feeling desolated.

Francis did not like long periods of silence. To lighten the gloom, he said, in a voice not devoid of cheer: "You're quite right. I knew this was coming. A little parting is probably in order. It's always done us good in the past."

"I think this should not be a little parting," said Billy, whose command over her voice was far from total. Their previous separations had lasted a month at best.

"It's probably for the best," Francis finally said. "I guess this couldn't go on indefinitely." He did not say it with conviction.

The raw weather had turned to rain. Francis and Billy sat on the sofa side by side in the dim light. Love made strange bedfellows, Billy thought, and then did absolutely nothing to help them out.

Five miles off the country blacktop was the dirt road called Old Wall Lane. It began in the state forest and ended on the border of old Mrs. Stern's property. Grey felt there were two ways to take this road: to whip around its corners at rather high speed raising a cloud of dust, or to slide down it in neutral since it was downhill all the way. Grey took the gentle course.

Halfway down, he stopped the car.

"Head out and up," he said. "Quick!"

They unrolled their windows and stuck their heads out. Sailing toward them was a red-tailed hawk. It floated over the car, low enough to see its speckled breast. The sight of a hawk up close always made Billy's heart pound. She and Grey, each autumn, climbed Mirage Mountain in western Connecticut to watch the annual hawk migration. It was a childhood longing of Grey's to own and train a kestrel, and for their first wedding anniversary, Billy had gotten him a first edition of *The Goshawk*.

At the bottom of the road was Wall Swamp, where Grey had proposed. Since then they had explored the swamp extensively by canoe. Grey stopped the car and got out to stretch his legs. Billy got out, too.

"Don't crush me," she said as Grey put his arm around her. They embraced as from a distance so as not to mess up Billy's dress.

"This is a pretty fancy business," Grey said. "Not like *our* wedding." Billy and Grey had gotten married in London, with their parents and siblings as witnesses in a registry office, and, after lunch, taken off in a rented car and driven to Dorset to explore the coast and search for anomites and other fossils.

"I like ours better," Billy said. "I actually don't care if this dress gets creased."

They stood in the middle of the road, closed their eyes, and kissed like teenagers.

Parting had been the sensible thing to do. A love affair could be compared to a cellar hole. Old Mrs. Stern's property had several such holes, remnants of eighteenth-century households. After a long while, without a map of the property, it was impossible to tell where they were. Standing on a road kissing your husband, taking the car to be serviced, letters, meals, telephone calls, arrangements, and errands filled up the hole of a love affair so well that after a while it would be possible to stand comfortably on top of it.

.   .   .

A tent had been pitched on the lawn next to the house. As they drove up the long driveway, Billy could see waiters with baskets of flowers dressing the tables. Penny's mother stood in the center of the tent wearing a lilac dress and directing waiters and maids.

On the steps of the house stood Penny's grandmother, the ferocious old Mrs. Stern. She had declared that this would be the last wedding she would live to see, but she looked far from frail. She was a stout old lady with white hair and stark, piercing blue eyes. She wore a yellow dress and leaned on a cane that looked more like a bishop's crozier, an effect of which she was not unaware.

"Josephine, my dear one," she said, clutching Billy's hand. "And Grey. How lovely to see you so nice and early. Have you had breakfast? No? Well, Grey, do go sit with David. He's all alone and lonely in the sun room. No one is paying any attention to him at all. As for you, my dearest, go instantly up to Penny, who is having some sort of nervous crisis. She sent her father down to the pharmacy to buy some emery boards, and she knows perfectly well that we have dozens of them in the supply cupboard. Oh, well. She hasn't had breakfast. Do make her eat."

Upstairs in her childhood bedroom, Penny sat in her long white wedding dress, staring into the dressing table mirror. A wreath of flowers hung over the back of the chair. Penny was tall and pale, and she wore her pale hair pulled back in a chignon. She and Billy had been friends since they were ten. In the summer, both families came home to America for a holiday, and Billy and Penny always spent a month together at old Mrs. Stern's. In this room they had sneaked cigarettes, drunk purloined beer, read love comics, written unsent love letters, plotted revenge on their school enemies, and read under the covers with flashlights after they had been told to go to sleep.

"Is David still alive?" she said to Billy by way of greeting.

"I'm afraid he's dead," said Billy. "The wedding is off. Here's a cigarette."

"What a relief," said Penny. "God, this is hell. This would never have happened if we had been allowed to run off to city hall like you guys."

"Oh, come on," Billy said. "You wanted to get married here. Besides, your gran says it's her last wedding."

"She's been saying that for thirty years," said Penny. "She'll be saying that when my as yet unborn children get married." She blew a smoke ring and watched it float toward the ceiling and dispel. She sighed. "The end of my girlhood. The end of all good things. Why am I doing this?"

"It's nice," said Billy. "It's not so bad."

Penny looked up. She was suddenly in a very dark mood. "*You're* a fine one to talk," she said.

"That's over," said Billy.

"Really?" Penny said. "You didn't tell me. Did it just happen?"

"It happened the day we went shopping, as a matter of fact," said Billy.

"Gee," Penny said. "Do you realize that the plans for this bloody wedding have kept me from having a real talk with my oldest friend? Or did you keep it from me."

"I kept it from you because I felt so awful," said Billy. "I felt awful about feeling awful. Now I feel very light and free and *right* and truly awful once in a while."

"You poor little duck," Penny said. "Hand me another of them smokes. Whether it's over or not is not the point. The point of course is that it existed at all. It proves *my* point: marriage is unlivable."

"He's a fine young laddie you're marrying."

"Really?" Penny said. "I can't seem to stand the thought of him at the moment."

A sweet breeze blew in through the window. Billy lit her cigarette and watched the breeze bat the smoke around. She and Penny never smoked except when they were together. It was a childhood tradition. Neither of them inhaled but both blew very beautiful smoke rings, a skill they had been perfecting for years.

"Did you feel sick on your wedding day?" asked Penny.

"I can't remember," said Billy. "But I don't think so. After all, I didn't have to go through all this."

"I wasn't at your wedding," Penny said gloomily.

"I noticed that."

"I'll never forgive myself," Penny said.

"If you remember correctly," Billy said, "you were taking exams and it was *very* spur-of-the-moment. You did, however, throw us a big party."

"I will never forgive myself for not seeing your sickly, ashy face on the morning of your wedding. God, this dress is uncomfortable. I now see why you hate clothes. By the way, they won't let me wear a watch in this getup. What's the time?"

"You have forty minutes before they throw the switch," said Billy. "Do you require a last meal?"

"I'm starving, now that you mention it," Penny said. "Bring me something. Toast. Coffee. Anything."

Billy returned with a tray of coffee, buttered toast, and some cheese puffs stolen off the caterer's tray, along with two oversized linen napkins provided by Penny's mother lest the bride get crumbs or butter on her dress.

"What's going on down there?" Penny said.

"People keep showing up. Grey and David are planning a fishing trip. Your father forgot the emery boards and says they're not necessary anyway. Hawks and Ricardo are here chatting up your gran."

Dr. Hawks was the local Congregationalist minister and Dr. Ricardo was the rabbi of Mrs. Stern's New York congregation. They would jointly perform the ceremony.

"I could eat fifteen times this much toast," said Penny. "These cheese puffs are top rate. I don't suppose you'd hop downstairs and get more."

"I have strict instructions not to bring you anything else."

Penny sighed and sipped her coffee. "I'll be very happy once this is over. I have to keep remembering that it only lasts a couple of hours."

"It lasts a lifetime," Billy said.

"There's always divorce, my girl," said Penny. "Is your entanglement really over?"

"It better be," Billy said. "When I look back over the last two years, I can't believe the person who lived that life is me. You can't imagine how exotic I felt to myself. I never had interesting romances like you. *That* was my interesting romance. I thought if I gave it up I would be my same old self, but I seem to be some other old self."

In Penny's room Billy was her old self. Francis did not know anything about her real life, her past, her childhood. They were each other's exception, and had nothing to do with each other at all.

"You'll get over it," said Penny.

"That doesn't seem to matter," Billy said. "Maybe I will and maybe I won't. But now it's part of me. It's history. It's my own historical event. In some way it doesn't matter what I *feel*. It's what I remember."

After the ceremony, the party sat down to lunch. Waiters hovered with trays of champagne. Plates were filled, emptied, refilled, and taken away. The three-tiered cake was cut amidst cheers and toasts. Between courses, the bride and groom tablehopped, making sure they talked to everyone.

Right before the ceremony Billy had switched the place cards so she and Grey could sit together. This did not go unnoticed

by old Mrs. Stern, who did not like things to be changed without her say-so, but Billy and Grey were exempt. Billy took
Grey's hand under the table. The ceremony, unlike their own
spare vows, had affected them both. They sat with their knees
touching. Billy felt as if she had been on a long, perilous jour-
ney and had come back with a grateful heart to everything she
belonged to.

When the waiters appeared with coffee, Penny knocked
Billy's elbow.

"Let's go for a ride," she said.

Arm in arm they ran down the hill through the apple or-
chard, through a gate in the low stone wall and past the rock
garden. Penny wound her wedding dress around her middle. On
the bank of the pond lying on its back like a giant turtle in the
sun was the Old Town canoe Penny and Billy had played Indian
scouts in as children.

Billy flipped the canoe over. "I've splattered my dress," she
said.

"It's only water," Penny said. "It won't stain."

They hiked up their skirts, slipped off their shoes, and Penny
hopped in. Billy gave the canoe a shove and jumped in too.

"I filched a couple of cigs," said Billy, taking one from behind
each ear. She had stuck a pack of matches into her bra.

They paddled across the pond. There, beside a willow, they
stopped and lit their cigarettes.

"Do you think they think we've bolted?" Penny said.

"They think we're going for a spin. Your grandmother waved
to us," Billy said.

"Then they probably think this is some charming part of the
day's events," Penny said.

"It is, isn't it?"

"This is the end of my girlhood," Penny said again glumly.

"We haven't been girls for years," said Billy.

They sat smoking and watching the water spiders jump from

ripple to ripple. There was an occasional flutter on the surface as a brown trout rose to snap at a mayfly.

Across the pond, the house sat securely on its rise, a big white and yellow clapboard house with six chimneys. From a distance it looked secure, remote. If she squinted Billy could see Grey talking to Penny's father.

The sun came through the willow branches speckling the water with light. Billy could have conjured up Francis in a flash if she had wanted to. She could have imagined him sitting on the bank waiting for her to float back to him.

"I guess we've had it," Penny said. "I mean we ought to paddle home." She sighed. "Doesn't everything feel *unknown* to you?"

"It's as plain as the nose on your face," Billy said.

"I feel as if life is all spread out in front of me but I don't know what's there," said Penny.

"That's what life is like," Billy said.

They flicked their cigarettes into the water and, sitting up straight as Indian scouts with their wedding clothes billowing behind them, they paddled back, shooting across the water in that swift, determined way of long ago.

Another Marvelous Thing

On a cold, rainy morning in February, Billy Delielle stood by the window of her hospital room looking over Central Park. She was a week and a half from the time her baby was due to be born, and she had been put into the hospital because her blood pressure had suddenly gone up and her doctor wanted her constantly monitored and on bed rest.

A solitary jogger in bright red foul-weather gear ran slowly down the glistening path. The trees were black and the branches were bare. There was not another soul out. Billy had been in the hospital for five days. The first morning she had woken to the sound of squawking. Since her room was next door to the nursery, she assumed this was a sound some newborns made. The next day she got out of bed at dawn and saw that the meadow was full of sea gulls who congregated each morning before the sun came up.

The nursery was an enormous room painted soft yellow. When Billy went to take the one short walk a day allowed her, she found herself averting her eyes from the neat rows of babies in their little plastic bins, but once in a while she found herself hungry for the sight of them. Taped to each crib was a blue (I'M A BOY) or pink (I'M A GIRL) card telling mother's name, the time of birth, and birth weight.

At six in the morning the babies were taken to their mothers to be fed. Billy was impressed by the surprising range of noises they made: mewing, squawking, bleating, piping, and squealing. The fact that she was about to have one of these creatures herself filled her with a combination of bafflement, disbelief, and longing.

For the past two months her chief entertainment had been to lie in bed and observe her unborn child moving under her skin. It had knocked a paperback book off her stomach and caused the saucer of her coffee cup to jiggle and dance.

Billy's husband, Grey, was by temperament and inclination a naturalist. Having a baby was right up his street. Books on neonatology and infant development replaced the astronomy and bird books on his night table. He gave up reading mysteries for texts on childbirth. One of these books had informed him that babies can hear in the womb, so each night he sang "Roll Along Kentucky Moon" directly into Billy's stomach. Another suggested that the educational process could begin before birth. Grey thought he might try to teach the unborn to count.

"Why stop there?" Billy said. "Teach it fractions."

Billy had a horror of the sentimental. In secret, for she would rather have died than showed it, the thought of her own baby brought her to tears. Her dreams were full of infants. Babies appeared everywhere. The buses abounded with pregnant women. The whole process seemed to her one half miraculous and the other half preposterous. She looked around her on a crowded street and said to herself: "Every single one of these people was *born.*"

Her oldest friend, Penny Stern, said to her: "We all hope

that this pregnancy will force you to wear maternity clothes, because they will be so much nicer than what you usually wear." Billy went shopping for maternity clothes but came home empty-handed.

She said, "I don't wear puffed sleeves and frilly bibs and ribbons around my neck when I'm not pregnant, so I don't see why I should have to just because I am pregnant." In the end, she wore Grey's sweaters, and she bought two shapeless skirts with elastic waistbands. Penny forced her to buy one nice black dress, which she wore to teach her weekly class in economic history at the business school.

Grey set about renovating a small spare room that had been used for storage. He scraped and polished the floor, built shelves, and painted the walls pale apple green with the ceiling and moldings glossy white. They had once called this room the lumber room. Now they referred to it as the nursery. On the top of one of the shelves Grey put his collection of glass-encased bird's nests. He already had in mind a child who would go on nature hikes with him.

As for Billy, she grimly and without expression submitted herself to the number of advances science had come up with in the field of obstetrics.

It was possible to have amniotic fluid withdrawn and analyzed to find out the genetic health of the unborn and, if you wanted to know, its sex. It was possible to lie on a table and with the aid of an ultrasonic scanner see your unborn child in the womb. It was also possible to have a photograph of this view. As for Grey, he wished Billy could have a sonogram every week, and he watched avidly while Billy's doctor, a handsome, rather melancholy South African named Jordan Bell, identified a series of blobs and clouds as head, shoulders, and back.

Every month in Jordan Bell's office Billy heard the sound of her own child's heart through ultrasound and what she heard sounded like galloping horses in the distance.

Billy went about her business outwardly unflapped. She continued to teach and she worked on her dissertation. In between,
when she was not napping, she made lists of baby things: crib
sheets, a stroller, baby T-shirts, diapers, blankets. Two months
before the baby was due, she and Penny went out and bought
what was needed. She was glad she had not saved this until
the last minute, because in her ninth month, after an uneventful
pregnancy, she was put in the hospital, where she was allowed
to walk down the hall once a day. The sense of isolation she had
cherished—just herself, Grey, and their unborn child—was gone.
She was in the hands of nurses she had never seen before, and
she found herself desperate for their companionship because
she was exhausted, uncertain, and lonely in her hospital room.

Billy was admitted wearing the nice black dress Penny had
made her buy and taken to a private room that overlooked the
park. At the bottom of her bed were two towels and a hospital
gown that tied up the back. Getting undressed to go to bed in
the afternoon made her feel like a child forced to take a nap.
She did not put on the hospital gown. Instead, she put on the
plaid flannel nightshirt of Grey's that she had packed in her bag
weeks ago in case she went into labor in the middle of the
night.

"I hate it here already," Billy said.

"It's an awfully nice view," Grey said. "If it were a little further along in the season I could bring my field glasses and see
what's nesting."

"I'll never get out of here," Billy said.

"Not only will you get out of here," said Grey, "you will be
released a totally transformed woman. You heard Jordan—all
babies get born one way or another."

If Grey was frightened, he never showed it. Billy knew that
his way of dealing with anxiety was to fix his concentration, and
it was now fixed on her and on being cheerful. He had never
seen Billy so upset before. He held her hand.

"Don't worry," he said. "Jordan said this isn't serious. It's just a complication. The baby will be fine and you'll be fine. Besides, it won't know how to be a baby and we won't know how to be parents."

Grey had taken off his jacket and he felt a wet place where Billy had laid her cheek. He did not know how to comfort her.

"A mutual learning experience," Billy said into his arm. "I thought nature was supposed to take over and do all this for us."

"It will," Grey said.

Seven o'clock began visiting hours. Even with the door closed Billy could hear shrieks and coos and laughter. With her door open she could hear champagne corks being popped.

Grey closed the door. "You didn't eat much dinner," he said. "Why don't I go downstairs to the delicatessen and get you something?"

"I'm not hungry," Billy said. She did not know what was in front of her, or how long she would be in this room, or how and when the baby would be born.

"I'll call Penny and have her bring something," Grey said.

"I already talked to her," Billy said. "She and David are taking you out to dinner." David was Penny's husband, David Hooks.

"You're trying to get rid of me," Grey said.

"I'm not," Billy said. "You've been here all day, practically. I just want the comfort of knowing that you're being fed and looked after. I think you should go soon."

"It's too early," said Grey. "Fathers don't have to leave when visiting hours are over."

"You're not a father yet," Billy said. "Go."

After he left she waited by the window to watch him cross the street and wait for the bus. It was dark and cold and it had begun to sleet. When she saw him she felt pierced with desolation. He was wearing his old camel's hair coat and the wind blew through his wavy hair. He stood back on his heels as he

had as a boy. He turned around and scanned the building for
her window. When he saw her, he waved and smiled. Billy
waved back. A taxi, thinking it was being hailed, stopped. Grey
got in and was driven off.

Every three hours a nurse appeared to take her temperature,
blood pressure, and pulse. After Grey had gone, the night nurse
appeared. She was a tall, middle-aged black woman named
Mrs. Perch. In her hand she carried what looked like a suitcase
full of dials and wires.

"Don't be alarmed," Mrs. Perch said. She had a soft West
Indian accent. "It is only a portable fetal heart monitor. You
get to say good morning and good evening to your baby."

She squirted a blob of cold blue jelly on Billy's stomach and
pushed a transducer around in it, listening for the beat. At once
Billy heard the sound of galloping hooves. Mrs. Perch timed
the beats against her watch.

"Nice and healthy," Mrs. Perch said.

"Which part of this baby is where?" Billy said.

"Well, his head is back here, and his back is there and
here is the rump and his feet are near your ribs. Or hers, of
course."

"I wondered if that was a foot kicking," Billy said.

"My second boy got his foot under my rib and kicked with
all his might," Mrs. Perch said.

Billy sat up in bed. She grabbed Mrs. Perch's hand. "Is this
baby going to be all right?" she said.

"Oh my, yes," Mrs. Perch said. "You're not a very interesting
case. Many others much more complicated than you have done
very well and you will, too."

At four in the morning, another nurse appeared, a florid
Englishwoman. Billy had spent a restless night, her heart
pounding, her throat dry.

"Your pressure's up, dear," said the nurse, whose tag read
"M. Whitely." "Dr. Bell has written orders that if your pres-

sure goes up you're to have a shot of hydralazine. It doesn't hurt baby—did he explain that to you?"

"Yes," said Billy groggily.

"It may give you a little headache."

"What else?"

"That's all," Miss Whitely said.

Billy fell asleep and woke with a pounding headache. When she rang the bell, the nurse who had admitted her appeared. Her name was Bonnie Near and she was Billy's day nurse. She gave Billy a pill and then taped a tongue depressor wrapped in gauze over her bed.

"What's that for?" Billy said.

"Don't ask," said Bonnie Near.

"I want to know."

Bonnie Near sat down at the end of the bed. She was a few years older than Billy, trim and wiry with short hair and tiny diamond earrings.

"It's hospital policy," she said. "The hydralazine gives you a headache, right? You ring to get something to make it go away and because you have high blood pressure everyone assumes that the blood pressure caused it, not the drug. So this thing gets taped above your bed in the one chance in about fifty-five million that you have a convulsion."

Billy turned her face away and stared out the window.

"Hey, hey," said Bonnie Near. "None of this. I noticed yesterday that you're quite a worrier. Are you like this when you're not in the hospital? Listen. I'm a straight shooter and I would tell you if I was worried about you. I'm not. You're just the common garden variety."

Every morning Grey appeared with two cups of coffee and the morning paper. He sat in a chair and he and Billy read the paper together as they did at home.

"Is the house still standing?" Billy asked after several days. "Are the banks open? Did you bring the mail? I feel I've been here ten months instead of a week."

"The mail was very boring," Grey said. "Except for this booklet from the Wisconsin Loon Society. You'll be happy to know that you can order a record called 'Loon Music.' Would you like a copy?"

"If I moved over," Billy said, "would you take off your jacket and lie down next to me?"

Grey took off his jacket and shoes, and curled up next to Billy. He pressed his nose into her face and looked as if he could drift off to sleep in a second.

"Childworld called about the crib," he said into her neck. "They want to know if we want white paint or natural pine. I said natural."

"That's what I think I ordered," Billy said. "They let the husbands stay over in this place. They call them 'dads.'"

"I'm not a dad yet, as you pointed out," Grey said. "Maybe they'll just let me take naps here."

There was a knock on the door. Grey sprang to his feet and Jordan Bell appeared.

"Don't look so nervous, Billy," he said. "I have good news. I think we want to get this baby born if your pressure isn't going to go down. I think we ought to induce you."

Billy and Grey were silent.

"The way it works is that we put you on a drip of pitocin, which is a synthetic of the chemical your brain produces when you go into labor."

"We know," Billy said. "Katherine went over it in childbirth class." Katherine Walden was Jordan Bell's nurse. "When do you want to do this?"

"Tomorrow," Jordan Bell said. "Katherine will come over and give you your last Lamaze class right here."

"And if it doesn't work?"

"It usually does," said Jordan Bell. "And if it doesn't, we do a second-day induction."

"And if that doesn't work?"

"It generally does. If it doesn't, we do a cesarean, but you'll be awake and Grey can hold your hand."

"Oh what fun," said Billy.

When Jordan Bell left, Billy burst into tears.

"Why isn't anything normal?" she said. "Why do I have to lie here day after day listening to other people's babies crying? Why is my body betraying me like this?"

Grey kissed her and then took her hands. "There is no such thing as normal," he said. "Everyone we've talked to has some story or other—huge babies that won't budge, thirty-hour labors. A cesarean is a perfectly respectable way of being born."

"What about me? What about me getting all stuck up with tubes and cut up into little pieces?" Billy said, and she was instantly ashamed. "I hate being like this. I feel I've lost myself and some whimpering, whining person has taken me over."

"Think about how in two months we'll have a two-month-old baby to take to the park."

"Do you really think everything is going to be all right?" Billy said.

"Yes," said Grey. "I do. In six months we'll be in Maine."

Billy lay in bed with her door closed reading her brochure from the Loon Society. She thought about the cottage she and Grey rented every August in Jewell Neck, Maine, on a lagoon. There at night with blackness all around them and not a light to be seen, they heard hoot owls and loons calling their night cries to one another. Loon mothers carried their chicks on their back, Billy knew. The last time she had heard those cries she had been just three months pregnant. The next time she heard them she would have a child.

She thought about the baby shower Penny had given her—a lunch party for ten women. At the end of it, Billy and Grey's unborn child had received cotton and wool blankets, little sweaters, tiny garments with feet, and two splendid Teddy bears. The Teddy bears had sat on the coffee table. Billy remembered the strange, light feeling in her chest as she looked at them. She had picked them both up and laughed with astonishment.

At a red light on the way home in a taxi, surrounded by boxes and bags of baby presents, she saw something that made her heart stop: Francis Clemens, who for two years had been Billy's illicit lover.

With the exception of her family, Billy was close only to Grey and Penny Stern. She had never been the subject of anyone's romantic passion. She and Grey, after all, had been fated to marry. She had loved him all her life.

Francis had pursued her: no one had ever pursued her before. The usual signs of romance were as unknown to Billy as the workings of a cyclotron. Crushes, she had felt, were for children. She did not really believe that adults had them.

Without her knowing it, she was incubating a number of curious romantic diseases. One day when Francis came to visit wearing his tweed coat and the ridiculously long paisley scarf he affected, she realized that she had fallen in love.

The fact of Francis was the most exotic thing that had ever happened in Billy's fairly stolid, uneventful life. He was as brilliant as a painted bunting. He was also, in marked contrast to Billy, beautifully dressed. He did not know one tree from another. He felt all birds were either robins or crows. He was avowedly urban and his pleasures were urban. He loved opera, cocktail parties, and lunches. They did not agree about economic theory, either.

Nevertheless, they spent what now seemed to Billy an enormous amount of time together. She had not sought anything like this. If her own case had been presented to her she would have dismissed it as messy, unnecessary, and somewhat sordid, but when she fell in love she fell as if backward into a swimming pool. For a while she felt dazed. Then Francis became a fact in her life. But in the end she felt her life was being ruined.

She had not seen Francis for a long time. In that brief glance at the red light she saw his paisley scarf, its long fringes flapping in the breeze. It was amazing that someone who had been so close to her did not know that she was having a baby. As the cab pulled away, she did not look back at him. She stared rigidly frontward, flanked on either side by presents for her unborn child.

The baby kicked. Mothers-to-be should not be lying in hospital beds thinking about illicit love affairs, Billy thought. Of course, if you were like the other mothers on the maternity floor and probably had never had an illicit love affair, you would not be punished by lying in the hospital in the first place. You would go into labor like everyone else, and come rushing into Maternity Admitting with your husband and your suitcase. By this time tomorrow she would have her baby in her arms, just like everyone else, but she drifted off to sleep thinking of Francis nonetheless.

At six in the morning, Bonnie Near woke her.

"You can brush your teeth," she said. "But don't drink any water. And your therapist is here to see you, but don't be long."

The door opened and Penny walked in.

"And how are we today?" she said. "Any strange dreams or odd thoughts?"

"How did you get in here?" Billy said.

"I said I was your psychiatrist and that you were being induced today and so forth," Penny said. "I just came to say good luck. Here's all the change we had in the house. Tell Grey to call constantly. I'll see you all tonight."

Billy was taken to the labor floor and hooked up to a fetal heart monitor whose transducers were kept on her stomach by a large elastic cummerbund. A stylish-looking nurse wearing hospital greens, a string of pearls, and perfectly applied pink lipstick poked her head through the door.

"Hi!" she said in a bright voice. "I'm Joanne Kelly. You're my patient today." She had the kind of voice and smile Billy could not imagine anyone's using in private. "Now, how are we? Fine? All right. Here's what we're going to do. First of all, we're going to put this IV into your arm. It will only hurt a little and then we're going to hook you up to something called pitocin. Has Dr. Bell explained any of this to you?" Joanne Kelly said.

"All," said Billy.

"Neat," Joanne Kelly said. "We *like* an informed patient. Put your arm out, please."

Billy stuck out her arm. Joanne Kelly wrapped a rubber thong under her elbow.

"Nice veins," she said. "You would have made a lovely junkie.

"Now we're going to start the pitocin," Joanne Kelly said. "We start off slow to see how you do. Then we escalate." She looked Billy up and down. "Okay," she said. "We're off and running. Now, I've got a lady huffing and puffing in the next room so I have to go and coach her. I'll be back real soon."

Billy lay looking at the clock, or watching the pitocin and glucose drip into her arm. She could not get a comfortable position and the noise of the fetal heart monitor was loud and harsh. The machine itself spat out a continual line of data.

Jordan Bell appeared at the foot of her bed.

"An exciting day—yes, Billy?" he said. "What time is Grey coming?"

"I told him to sleep late," Billy said. "All the nurses told me that this can take a long time. How am I supposed to feel when it starts working?"

"If all goes well, you'll start to have contractions and then they'll get stronger and then you'll have your baby."

"Just like that?" said Billy.

"Pretty much just like that."

But by five o'clock in the afternoon nothing much had happened.

Grey sat in a chair next to the bed. From time to time he checked the data. He had been checking it all day.

"That contraction went right off the paper," he said. "What did it feel like?"

"Intense," Billy said. "It just doesn't hurt."

"You're still in the early stages," said Jordan Bell when he came to check her. "I'm willing to stay on if you want to continue, but the baby might not be born till tomorrow."

"I'm beat," said Billy.

"Here's what we can do," Jordan said. "We can keep going or we start again tomorrow."

"Tomorrow," said Billy.

She woke up exhausted with her head pounding. The sky was cloudy and the glare hurt her eyes. She was taken to a different labor room.

In the night her blood pressure had gone up. She had begged not to have a shot—she did not see how she could go into labor feeling so terrible, but the shot was given. It had been a long, sleepless night.

She lay alone with a towel covering one eye, trying to sleep, when a nurse appeared by her side. This one looked very young, had curly hair, and thick, slightly rose-tinted glasses. Her tag read "Eva Gottlieb." Underneath she wore a button inscribed EVA: WE DELIVER.

"Hi," said Eva Gottlieb. "I'm sorry I woke you, but I'm your nurse for the day and I have to get you started."

"I'm here for a lobotomy," Billy said. "What are you going to do to me?"

"I'm going to run a line in you," Eva Gottlieb said. "And then I don't know what. Because your blood pressure is high, I'm supposed to wait until Jordan gets here." She looked at Billy carefully. "I know it's scary," she said. "But the worst that can happen is that you have to be sectioned and that's not bad."

Billy's head throbbed.

"That's easy for you to say," she said. "I'm the section."

Eva Gottlieb smiled. "I'm a terrific nurse," she said. "I'll stay with you."

Tears sprang in Billy's eyes. "Why will you?"

"Well, first of all, it's my job," said Eva. "And second of all, you look like a reasonable person."

Billy looked at Eva carefully. She felt instant, total trust. Perhaps that was part of being in hospitals and having babies. Everyone you came in contact with came very close, very fast.

Billy's eyes hurt. Eva was hooking her up to the fetal heart monitor. Her touch was strong and sure, and she seemed to know Billy did not want to be talked to. She flicked the machine on, and Billy heard the familiar sound of galloping hooves.

"Is there any way to turn it down?" Billy said.

"Sure," said Eva. "But some people find it consoling."

As the morning wore on, Billy's blood pressure continued to rise. Eva was with her constantly.

"What are they going to do to me?" Billy asked.

"I think they're probably going to give you magnesium sulfate to get your blood pressure down and then they're going to section you. Jordan does a gorgeous job, believe me. I won't let them do anything to you without explaining it first, and if you get out of bed first thing tomorrow and start moving around you'll be fine."

Twenty minutes later, a doctor Billy had never seen before administered a dose of magnesium sulfate.

"Can't you do this?" Billy asked Eva.

"It's heavy-duty stuff," Eva said. "It has to be done by a doctor."

"Can they wait until my husband gets here?"

"It's too dangerous," said Eva. "It has to be done. I'll stay with you."

The drug made her hot and flushed, and brought her blood pressure straight down. For the next hour, Billy tried to sleep. She had never been so tired. Eva brought her cracked ice to suck on and a cloth for her head. The baby wiggled and writhed, and the fetal heart monitor gauged its every move. Finally, Grey and Jordan Bell were standing at the foot of her bed.

"Okay, Billy," said Jordan. "Today's the day. We must get the baby out. I explained to Grey about the mag sulfate. We both agree that you must have a cesarean."

"When?" Billy said.

"In the next hour," said Jordan. "I have to check two patients and then we're off to the races."

"What do you think," Billy asked Grey.

"It's right," Grey said.

"And what about you?" Billy said to Eva.

"It has to be done," Eva said.

Jordan Bell was smiling a genuine smile and he looked dashing and happy.

"Why is he so uplifted?" Billy asked Eva after he had dashed down the hall.

"He loves the OR," she said. "He loves deliveries. Think of it this way: you're going to get your baby at last."

. . .

Billy lay on a gurney, waiting to be rolled down the hall. Grey, wearing hospital scrubs, stood beside her holding her hand. She had been prepped and given an epidural anesthetic, and she could no longer feel her legs.

"Look at me," she said to Grey. "I'm a mass of tubes. I'm a miracle of modern science." She put his hand over her eyes.

Grey squatted down to put his head near hers. He looked expectant, exhausted, and worried, but when he saw her scanning his face he smiled.

"It's going to be swell," Grey said. "We'll find out if it's little William or little Ella."

Billy's heart was pounding but she thought she ought to say something to keep her side up. She said, "I knew we never should have had sexual intercourse." Grey gripped her hand tight and smiled. Eva laughed. "Don't you guys leave me," Billy said.

Billy was wheeled down the hall by an orderly. Grey held one hand, Eva held the other. Then they left her to scrub.

She was taken to a large, pale green room. Paint was peeling on the ceiling in the corner. An enormous lamp hung over her head. The anesthetist appeared and tapped her feet.

"Can you feel this?" he said.

"It doesn't feel like feeling," Billy said. She was trying to keep her breathing steady.

"Excellent," he said.

Then Jordan appeared at her feet, and Grey stood by her head.

Eva bent down. "I know you'll hate this, but I have to tape your hands down, and I have to put this oxygen mask over your face. It comes off as soon as the baby's born, and it's good for you and the baby."

Billy took a deep breath. The room was very hot. A screen was placed over her chest.

"It's so you can't see," said Eva. "Here's the mask. I know it'll freak you out, but just breathe nice and easy. Believe me, this is going to be fast."

Billy's arms were taped, her legs were numb, and a clear plastic mask was placed over her nose and mouth. She was so frightened she wanted to cry out, but it was impossible. Instead she breathed as Katherine Walden had taught her to. Every time a wave of panic rose, she breathed it down. Grey held her hand. His face was blank and his glasses were fogged. His hair was covered by a green cap and his brow was wet. There was nothing she could do for him, except squeeze his hand.

"Now, Billy," said Jordan Bell, "you'll feel something cold on your stomach. I'm painting you with Betadine. All right, here we go."

Billy felt something like dull tugging. She heard the sound of foamy water. Then she felt the baby being slipped from her. She turned to Grey. His glasses had unfogged and his eyes were round as quarters. She heard a high, angry scream.

"Here's your baby," said Jordan Bell. "It's a beautiful, healthy boy."

Eva lifted the mask off Billy's face.

"He's perfectly healthy," Eva said. "Listen to those lungs." She took the baby to be weighed and tested. Then she came back to Billy. "He's perfect but he's little—just under five pounds. We have to take him upstairs to the preemie nursery. It's policy when they're not five pounds."

"Give him to me," Billy said. She tried to free her hands but they were securely taped.

"I'll bring him to you," Eva said. "But he can't stay down here. He's too small. It's for the baby's safety, I promise you. Look, here he is."

The baby was held against her forehead. The moment he came near her he stopped shrieking. He was mottled and wet.

"Please let me have him," Billy said.

"He'll be fine," Eva said. They then took him away.

The next morning Billy rang for the nurse and demanded that her IV be disconnected. Twenty minutes later she was out of bed slowly walking.

"I feel as if someone had crushed my pelvic bones," Billy said.

"Someone did," said the nurse.

Two hours later she was put into a wheelchair and pushed by a nurse into the elevator and taken to the Infant Intensive Care Unit. At the door the nurse said, "I'll wheel you in."

"I can walk," Billy said. "But thank you very much."

Inside, she was instructed to scrub with surgical soap and to put on a sterile gown. Then she walked very slowly and very stiffly down the hall. A Chinese nurse stopped her.

"I'm William Delielle's mother," she said. "Where is he?"

The nurse consulted a clipboard and pointed Billy down a hallway. Another nurse in a side room pointed to an isolette— a large plastic case with porthole windows. There on a white cloth lay her child.

He was fast asleep, his little arm stretched in front of him, an exact replica of Grey's sleeping posture. On his back were two discs the size of nickels hooked up to wires that measured his temperature and his heart and respiration rates on a console above his isolette. He was long and skinny and beautiful.

"He looks like a little chicken," said Billy. "May I hold him?"

"Oh, no," said the nurse. "Not for a while. He mustn't be stressed." She gave Billy a long look and said, "But you can open the windows and touch him."

Billy opened the porthole window and touched his leg. He shivered slightly. She wanted to disconnect his probes, scoop him up, and hold him next to her. She stood quietly, her hand resting lightly on his calf.

The room was bright, hot, and busy. Nurses came and went, washing their hands, checking charts, making notes, diapering, changing bottles of glucose solution. There were three other children in the room. One was very tiny and had a miniature IV attached to a vein in her head. A pink card was taped on her isolette. Billy looked on the side of William's isolette. There was a blue card and in Grey's tiny printing was written "William Delielle."

Later in the morning, when Grey appeared in her room he found Billy sitting next to a glass-encased pump.

"This is the well-known electric breast pump. Made in Switzerland," Billy said.

"It's like the medieval clock at Salisbury Cathedral," Grey said, peering into the glass case. "I just came from seeing William. He's much *longer* than I thought. I called all the grandparents. In fact, I was on the telephone all night after I left you." He gave her a list of messages. "They're feeding him in half an hour."

Billy looked at her watch. She had been instructed to use the pump for three minutes on each breast to begin with. Her milk, however, would not be given to William, who, the doctors said, was too little to nurse. He would be given carefully measured formula, and Billy would eventually have to wean him from the bottle and onto herself. The prospect of this seemed very remote.

As the days went by, Billy's room filled with flowers, but she spent most of her time in the Infant ICU. She could touch William but not hold him. The morning before she was to be discharged, Billy went to William's eight o'clock feeding. She thought how lovely it would be to feed him at home, how they might sit in the rocking chair and watch the birds in the garden below. In William's present home, there was no morning and no night. He had never been in a dark room, or heard bird sounds or traffic noise, or felt a cool draft.

William was asleep on his side wearing a diaper and a little T-shirt. The sight of him seized Billy with emotion.

"You can hold him today," the nurse said.

"Yes?"

"Yes, and you can feed him today, too."

Billy bowed her head. She took a steadying breath. "How can I hold him with all this hardware on him?" she said.

"I'll show you," said the nurse. She disconnected the console, reached into the isolette, and gently untaped William's probes. Then she showed Billy how to change him, put on his T-shirt, and swaddle him in a cotton blanket. In an instant he was in Billy's arms.

He was still asleep, but he made little screeching noises and wrinkled his nose. He moved against her and nudged his head into her arm. The nurse led her to a rocking chair and for the first time she sat down with her baby.

All around her, lights blazed. The radio was on and a sweet male voice sang, "I want you to be mine, I want you to be mine, I want to take you home, I want you to be mine."

William opened his eyes and blinked. Then he yawned and began to cry.

"He's hungry," the nurse said, putting a small bottle into Billy's hand.

She fed him and burped him, and then she held him in her arms and rocked him to sleep. In the process she fell asleep, too, and was woken by the nurse and Grey, who had come from work.

"You must put him back now," said the nurse. "He's been out a long time and we don't want to stress him."

"It's awful to think that being with his mother creates stress," Billy said.

"Oh, no!" the nurse said. "That's not what I mean. I mean, in his isolette it's temperature controlled."

Once Billy was discharged from the hospital she had to commute to see William. She went to the two morning feedings, came home for a nap, and met Grey for the five o'clock. They raced out for dinner and came back for the eight. Grey would not let Billy stay for the eleven.

Each morning she saw Dr. Edmunds, the head of neonatology. He was a tall, slow-talking, sandy-haired man with horn-rimmed glasses.

"I know you will never want to hear this under any other circumstances," he said to Billy, "but your baby is very boring."

"How boring?"

"Very boring. He's doing just what he ought to do." William had gone to the bottom of his growth curve and was beginning to gain. "As soon as he's a little fatter he's all yours."

Billy stood in front of his isolette watching William sleep.

"This is like having an affair with a married man," Billy said to the nurse who was folding diapers next to her.

The nurse looked at her uncomprehendingly.

"I mean you love the person but can only see him at certain times," said Billy.

The nurse was young and plump. "I guess I see what you mean," she said.

At home William's room was waiting. The crib had been delivered and put together by Grey. While Billy was in the hospital, Grey had finished William's room. The Teddy bears sat on the shelves. A mobile of ducks and geese hung over the crib. Grey had bought a secondhand rocking chair and had painted it red. Billy had thought she would be unable to face William's empty room. Instead she found she could scarcely stay out of it. She folded and refolded his clothes, reorganized his drawers, arranged his crib blankets. She decided what should be his homecoming clothes and set them out on the changing table along with a cotton receiving blanket and a wool shawl.

But even though he did not look at all fragile and he was beginning to gain weight, it often felt to Billy that she would never have him. She and Grey had been told ten days to two weeks from day of birth. One day when she felt she could not stand much more Billy was told that she might try nursing him.

Touch him on his cheek. He will turn to you. Guide him toward the breast and the magical connection will be made.

Billy remembered this description from her childbirth books. She had imagined a softly lit room, a sense of peacefulness, some soft, sweet music in the background.

She was put behind a screen in William's room, near an isolette containing an enormous baby who was having breathing difficulties.

She was told to keep on her sterile gown, and was given sterile water to wash her breasts with. At the sight of his mother's naked bosom, William began to howl. The sterile gown dropped onto his face. Billy began to sweat. All around her, the nurses chatted, clattered, and dropped diapers into metal bins and slammed the tops down.

"Come on, William," Billy said. "The books say that this is the blissful union of mother and child."

But William began to scream. The nurse appeared with the formula bottle and William instantly stopped screaming and began to drink happily.

"Don't worry," the nurse said. "He'll catch on."

At night at home she sat by the window. She could not sleep. She had never felt so separated from anything in her life. Grey, to distract himself, was stenciling the wall under the molding in William's room. He had found an early American design of wheat and cornflowers. He stood on a ladder in his blue jeans carefully applying the stencil in pale blue paint.

One night Billy went to the door of the baby's room to watch him, but Grey was not on the ladder. He was sitting in the rocking chair with his head in his hands. His shoulders were shaking slightly. He had the radio on, and he did not hear her.

He had been so brave and cheerful. He had held her hand while William was born. He had told her it was like watching a magician sawing his wife in half. He had taken photos of William in his isolette and sent them to their parents and all their friends. He had read up on growth curves and had bought Billy a book on breast-feeding. He had also purloined his hospital greens to wear each year on William's birthday. Now *he* had broken down.

She made a noise coming into the room and then bent down and stroked his hair. He smelled of soap and paint thinner. She put her arms around him, and she did not let go for a long time.

Three times a day, Billy tried to nurse William behind a screen and each time she ended up giving him his formula.

Finally she asked a nurse, "Is there some room I could sit in alone with this child?"

"We're not set up for it," the nurse said. "But I could put you in the utility closet."

There amidst used isolettes and cardboard boxes of sterile water, on the second try William nursed for the first time. She touched his cheek. He turned to her, just as it said in the book. Then her eyes crossed.

"Oh, my God!" she said.

A nurse walked in.

"Hurts, right?" she said. "Good for him. That means he's got it. It won't hurt for long."

At his evening feeding he howled again.

"The course of true love never did run smooth," said Grey. He and Billy walked slowly past the park on their way home. It was a cold, wet night.

"I am a childless mother," Billy said.

Two days later William was taken out of his isolette and put into a plastic bin. He had no temperature or heart probes, and Billy could pick him up without having to disconnect anything. At his evening feeding when the unit was quiet, she took him out in the hallway and walked up and down with him.

The next day she was greeted by Dr. Edmunds.

"I've just had a chat with your pediatrician," he said. "How would you like to take your boring baby home with you?"

"When?" said Billy.

"Right now, if you have his clothes," Dr. Edmunds said. "Dr. Jacobson will be up in a few minutes and can officially release him."

She ran down the hall and called Grey.

"Go home and get William's things," she said. "They're springing him. Come and get us."

"You mean we can just walk out of there with him?" Grey said. "I mean, just take him under our arm? He barely knows us."

"Just get here. And don't forget the blankets."

A nurse helped Billy dress William. He was wrapped in a green and white receiving blanket and covered in a white wool shawl. On his head was a blue and green knitted cap. It slipped slightly sideways, giving him a raffish look.

They were accompanied in the elevator by a nurse. It was hospital policy that a nurse hold the baby, and hand it over at the door.

It made Billy feel light-headed to be standing out of doors with her child. She felt she had just robbed a bank and got away with it.

In the taxi, Grey gave the driver their address.

"Not door to door," Billy said. "Can we get out at the avenue and walk down the street just like everyone else?"

When the taxi stopped, they got out carefully. The sky was full of silver clouds and the air was blustery and cold. William squinted at the light and wrinkled his nose.

Then, with William tight in Billy's arms, the three of them walked down the street just like everyone else.

A Couple of Old Flames

At the autumn cocktail party of the *American Economic Review,*
Billy Delielle ran smack into Francis Clemens, whom she had
not seen for two years. He was wearing one of his beautiful
tweed jackets, and the ridiculously long paisley scarf he affected
was wound around his neck. At his left was a hefty black man
wearing a white skull cap, striped trousers, and a long tan linen
shift.

On Francis's right was a girl so blond and pretty it caused
Billy, who was dark and plain, to blink. The girl wore a fuzzy
red sweater, dangling earrings, and lipstick to match her nail
polish. She and Francis looked so wonderful together that it was
hard for Billy to believe that at one time Francis had been her
own illicit lover.

Billy was wearing her nine-month-old son, William, whom
she carried in a hip sling. He was a very cheerful baby who
clutched a rubber giraffe in one hand and a teething biscuit in
the other. Crumbs from his biscuit ornamented his mother's
skirt.

Francis came right over and gave them a hard stare. He looked almost angry. Before Billy could stop herself, she blurted: "Who's the dish?"

Francis's features instantly relaxed. A smile lit his face.

"That's Dr. Milton Obutu," he said. "I know you've been reading his articles on the economic history of the developing nations with avid interest."

"The other one."

"Oh," Francis said blithely. "A recent acquisition. Speaking of which, you seem to have acquired a little something yourself."

"This is my son, William," Billy said. "He's nine months old."

Francis leaned over and peered at William, who hid his face in his mother's neck.

"Not very friendly," Francis said.

"Don't be shy, Will," Billy said. "Show your face, please."

William looked up, smiled, and began to spit.

"He has your social style, I see," said Francis. "What a very good-looking boy."

"He looks like his father."

"He looks like you," Francis said. "Of course, I am less intimately connected with the way his father looks."

Billy felt her cheeks flush.

"So," she said. "I see you've found my replacement. A much better model and much nicer colors."

The beautiful blond girl was deep in conversation with Dr. Obutu. Her hair was swept up in a French twist and she wore an enormous gold bracelet.

"How interesting that after throwing me over you're actually jealous," said Francis.

Billy found she could not look Francis in the eye.

"Dr. Obutu looks very familiar," she said. "Did he win a prize or something?"

"I see motherhood has not made you any keener on current events," said Francis. "He won the Welch-Orlovsky Medal in

economics. A neat change of subject. I never knew that jealousy
was included in your emotional repertoire. Of course, I had no
idea you were fixing to have a baby. How little we know!"

This, of course, was not true: they had known dozens of
things. Billy felt her head cluttered with names of Francis's
friends, his children's teachers in high school and professors at
college, of Vera's clients, of Francis's former colleagues. She had
heard countless stories about his landlady in the South of France,
and in fact knew the history—that is, the history as Francis saw
it—of this woman's marriage, and so on.

Billy, on the other hand, was so unforthcoming that Francis
had given in to snooping, but snooping around the Delielle
household did not reveal much. Billy and Grey were a pair of
minimalists. Furthermore, Billy felt it was a betrayal to tell
Francis anything whereas Francis took the opposite tack. Information *defused* things, he felt. If he nattered on endlessly about
his family, he could con himself into thinking that there was
nothing odd about the way he was feeling. As a consequence, he
sang like a canary.

The most fascinating subject was taboo. They did not discuss
the reason for their love affair or its effect on their lives. They
had broken up any number of times but the last parting had
been final. Billy, as was customary, did the initiating. She said,
with a tone of resolve in her voice Francis had never heard before, "My life is being ruined."

Naturally, she did not say how it was being ruined but Francis
knew the knell of finality when he heard it. He had been listening for it all along, and when it came he was not entirely un-
relieved. While his life was not being ruined, it was made complicated in a way he often found unbearable. Now he was used
to missing Billy. It was rather like a chronic pain of the lower
back. When he looked at her and her child, a feeling akin to
rage overtook him.

"I always said you'd leave me in the dust," he said.

Billy was silent.

"You threw me over," Francis said.

"I did not," Billy said. Francis was pleased to see that there were tears in her eyes. "We were bound to part, one way or the other."

"We were?" Francis said. "Not from where I sat."

"Come off it, Frank," said Billy. "I left you sitting right where you belong, in your ornamental house surrounded by your loving family and thousands of friends and relations."

At the sound of the sharp tone in his mother's voice, William began to fidget. "He's getting bored," Billy said. "I'm going to have to take him away soon."

"Fine," said Francis. "I'll take you both away for a drink, and we can continue this most inspiring conversation."

"What about your friend?"

"Ishbelle?" Francis said. "She's very enterprising. She's writing a profile of Dr. Obutu for the *Wall Street Journal*."

"Ishbelle?" said Billy.

"She's half English, half Dutch," Francis said.

"And won't she think it's odd that you're leaving with me?"

"I'll take care of it," Francis said. "Besides, you're a woman with a baby. What could be more safe and respectable?"

They ambled to the corner. Francis took her by the arm. The air was chilly and wet, and it was getting dark.

"Here we are," he said, leading her through a wooden door.

Billy had had hundreds of meals with Francis, mostly in out of the way delicatessens, Chinese restaurants, or coffee shops. Now she found herself in a bar full of polished blond wood, with a fire burning in the grate and fresh flowers in an ornamental urn.

"Do you come here often?" Billy said.

"Once in a while."

"We never went to such a nice place."

"Not for lack of trying," Francis said.

They took a table with a banquette. William's eyes were closed, so Billy spread a little blanket, unzipped his snowsuit, and set him down to take a nap. She took off his hat and kissed his hair.

"Ah, motherhood," Francis said. "How odd it looks on you. In the old days you used to throw your keys into the pocket of one of your hideous jackets and off we'd go. Now I see you carry a little mother bag, with a blanket inside, and probably diapers, toys, and bottles too. How well organized you've become! Why, just days ago, it seems, you allowed me to wonder what sort of child *we'd* produce."

Billy had very accurate recall and reminded Francis that this had been his exclusive fantasy.

"You played your own small part," Francis said.

"Stop trying to make me feel more awful than I feel, Frank."

"I don't believe you feel awful," Francis said. "You let me go without so much as a goddamned by-your-leave."

"We had a million by-your-leaves," Billy said. "Besides, you had your baby. In fact, you had two."

Francis looked at her with an expression Billy had often suffered as fatherly tenderness. It made her wince.

"All right," Francis said. "As long as you ditched me for family life, you may as well tell me about it. How did it go?"

Billy had heard Francis's birth stories countless times. His son Quentin had been born in Paris on New Year's Eve and the doctor had set off a bottle of champagne in the delivery room. Aaron was a labor so fast he had almost been born in a taxicab.

Billy told Francis how she had been hospitalized for toxemia two weeks before William's birth, and William had been born by cesarean section; how he had been slightly underweight and made to stay in the hospital for eight days after Billy was released. It had felt like eight months. Billy knew she had not

quite gotten over it, and she was reluctant to tell Francis anything at all, but once she started, she found she could not stop.
At one point Francis was amazed to see tears streak down her
cheeks. Francis leaned back in his chair and listened with no
particular expression on his face.

"And the baby's father?" he said conversationally.

"Are you referring to my husband, Grey?" Billy said.

"And what does he think of all this?" said Francis.

Billy gaped at him. Did he really want to hear her tell him
how wonderful and patient Grey had been, how he had taken a
month's leave of absence from work and had barely left her and
William except to run errands, how tender and besotted he was?

"He's an excellent father," she said.

"And you are finding motherhood very fulfilling?" Francis
said.

"It's very public."

"As opposed to your previous activities?"

"Quite," Billy said. "For instance, if I take William to the
bank and he begins to squall, at least three people give me advice—to feed him, to give him a toy, or prop him up in his
stroller. When I took *you* to the bank, no one told me those
things."

Francis sipped his drink in silence. "What a change," he said.
"No more charming dalliance in that nasty study of yours, which
I assume is now the child's room."

"It isn't," Billy said. "We had that spare room, which is
warmer than my study."

"A snug family group," Francis said.

"Oh, shut up, Frank," Billy said. "You're snug enough. Didn't
you used to drag me by the hair over to your little snuggery and
show me album after album of happy family portraits? Don't be
so mingy."

"I'm not mingy," Francis said. "Look, your baby is awake."

William looked up from the banquette. His cheek was pink

from sleeping on it. Billy took him into her arms. "You look like a hungry boy," she said.

Francis suddenly looked alarmed. "I don't suppose you're one of those nurse-your-baby-in-public types," he said.

"Yup. I am," Billy said. "But don't you worry. I've got a nice bottle in my bag."

The lights of the bar gave the room an orange glow. Billy bent over her baby, who drank his bottle peacefully and stared up at her. Her hair fell into her eyes, but she did not have a free hand to push it away. Francis restrained himself from doing it for her.

"From mistress to mother," he said. "A tender scene. I wonder what sort of parent you are. Probably no nonsense. Schedules, enforced naps, and so on."

Billy, who found the experience of having a baby exactly like being madly in love, looked at Francis.

"I only treated *you* that way," she said. "Actually, I'm a very indulgent mother."

"It's funny what we didn't know about one another," Francis said.

"It's entirely appropriate to the situation," said Billy.

"For instance, I never figured out you and Grey and your attitude toward money. He makes a lot, you're an economic historian, and neither of you seems to care much about it."

"You mean what it buys," said Billy.

"I do mean that," said Francis, who was interested in it for no other reason. How he and Vera loved things! English cars, early American sideboards, Swedish tables, trips to Mexico, houses in the South of France, cashmere jackets, kilim rugs.

"Grey sees it as an abstraction and I see it as a force of history," Billy said.

Francis sighed. So that was that!

William had finished his bottle and was sitting on his mother's lap trying to take all the silverware off the table. Billy reached into her bag and pulled out his rubber giraffe and a set of plastic keys. When they both looked up, Francis could see what a replica of his mother William was. Billy kissed her baby's neck and he began to laugh. A look Francis had never seen before appeared on Billy's face. Francis sighed. He felt weak and depleted as if after a long swim.

"It's time to go," Billy said.

"One more thing," said Francis. "I've always wanted to know. When you and I snuck off to Vermont for our little trip when Vera and Grey were away, what did you tell Grey?"

She looked suddenly so stricken that Francis realized their trip had been the occasion of the first lie Billy had ever told her husband.

"Never mind," he said.

Billy pushed the hair off her forehead. She felt rather exhausted herself. "Okay, William," she said. "It's time for the horrible torture of your snowsuit."

She set William down on the banquette and started with his feet. He began to fidget and squirm. Then he began to cry.

"They all hate this," Billy said to Francis.

"Ours didn't."

"Really," Billy said. "How totally unusual."

Finally William was bundled up and fastened into his hip carrier. Francis threw some money on the table and they walked into the street.

It was misty and dark; halos formed around the street lamps.

"It feels like snow," said Francis. "It's very odd seeing you." Billy was silent.

"Is it odd seeing me?" he asked.

"Yes," said Billy.

"What a rewarding conversationalist you are," Francis said. "I suppose now that you have so many motherly chores you no longer wonder what we were doing together."

"I think about it a lot," said Billy.

"And what brilliant thoughts have you come up with?"

"Love seeketh only self to please," Billy said.

Francis grabbed her arm. "What's that supposed to mean?" he said.

"It's a quote from William Blake," said Billy. "Now I get to ask you a question."

"Yes," said Francis. Billy had never really asked him anything at all.

"Where'd you get that paisley scarf?"

Francis felt as if the air had been let out of his tires. "Is that all you want to know?"

"Sort of."

"It belonged to Vera's grandfather, who was quite a dandy. I'd be happy to give it to you as a good-bye present. You can keep it for William, and I can say I lost it."

"Oh, no!" said Billy. "I always think of you in that scarf."

Finally the three of them reached the corner. Francis was about to hail a taxi when Billy clutched his arm. "Are you in love with that girl?" she said.

Francis spun around. "What's it to you?"

"I want to know," Billy said. Her voice was shaking.

Francis looked down at her intently.

"Are you?" Billy said. She was clutching his arm rather painfully.

"She's my daughter-in-law," Francis said. "Aaron got married last year."

Billy let go. Francis saw that her face was flooded with relief, which was instantly supplanted by anger.

"You bastard," she said. "Stringing me along like that." She felt tired and sad. So Aaron had gotten married and she had never known!

"It shouldn't make any difference to you one way or the other," Francis said. "Now that you're a respectable wife and mother."

"Are you in love with anyone else?"

Francis did not have to repress the desire to kiss her: it was not easy to contemplate kissing a woman who was holding a baby. Instead he hung his scarf around her neck and pulled her a little closer. William found this very entertaining and began to laugh.

"Does that mean that if I can't be in love with you, I can't be in love with anyone else?" he said.

"I didn't mean that," said Billy, slipping out from under the scarf.

"I think you did," said Francis. A few fine snowflakes began to fall. "I'll get you a taxi so your precious darling doesn't get wet."

Francis hailed a cab and opened the door. He bent to kiss Billy good-bye.

She ducked her head to get through the door, so instead of kissing Billy, Francis kissed William on the side of his head, and as he watched them drive away, he could still smell that clear, benign baby smell of talcum powder and biscuits.

The next day Billy and Penny Stern took William to the park. Penny, who was a month away from having her own baby, and her husband, David Hooks, were William's godparents.

The park was in the back of a private school and was open to local children. The walk was lined with hedge, and beyond a lawn were swings, baby swings, a play house, slides, and a jungle gym. In the center was one enormous old cherry tree used for climbing.

Penny pushed William in his stroller, and Billy ambled along.

"Do you realize," she said, "this time next year we'll both have children to take to the park?"

"I realize it but I don't believe it," Penny said. "I can't even believe how enormous William is."

"He looks more like Grey every day," said Billy.

"Not so," Penny said. "He looks just like you. Of course, you and Grey look alike, so it's hard to tell who William resembles most."

It took having a baby to see how true this was. Billy had spent countless nights nursing William to sleep in the red rocking chair trying to figure out how in this gigantic, overpopulated world you invariably found your true other: a person you could live with who even looked like you. Grey might have married someone else, or become an anthropologist and gone to Mozambique, or he might have gotten a job in Buenos Aires and the world would have swallowed him up. Instead, he was waiting for her, right where they had started out—in London, on a warm June night. She could not get over that she and Grey had created this remarkable child, who looked like both of them but also looked only like himself. Someday he would go off and find *his* other.

And where, Billy wondered as she walked, did Francis fit into this? The fact was, he didn't. He had never fit in at all. He and Billy had nothing in common and were as different as two people can be. Yet there was no denying they had fallen in love, a process as mysterious as creating a child out of two cells. A love affair was another amazing product of human ingeniousness, like art, like scholarship, like architecture. It was a created thing with rules, language, and reference. When it was finished it lived on in its artifacts: a million memories and gestures.

William cooed in his stroller. Soon he would learn to talk. It often seemed unfair to Billy that she and Grey had not known each other as babies. His first word, according to his mother, had been "boot." Since William had been born Billy had been through boxes of her own and Grey's baby pictures. As far as she could tell, they all looked like William.

These days William was her constant reference. She liked to

sit quite still and let her feelings for him run over her, like pure, warm, water. Early in the morning when William got up, she brought him into bed between her and Grey, and she often felt at once content and quite wild with happiness.

The park, when they got there, was full of children, but the baby swings were empty.

"Give that child to me," Penny said as Billy got William out of his stroller. "I need swinging practice."

Billy sat on a bench and watched a group of little boys climbing the cherry tree under a sky full of low, silver clouds. She watched her child being swung by her oldest friend. William loved the swing. He closed his eyes and shrieked with joy, revealing his four beautiful teeth. It seemed an instant ago he had been an infant. Soon he would be walking, talking, going to college and writing articles on third world economies, like Dr. Obutu. Or perhaps he would fulfill one of his father's secret desires and become either a marine biologist or a forest ranger. He would grow up, get married, and have a baby of his own. The baby on the swing would be a sweet, distant memory.

"We're bored," said Penny sitting down beside Billy. "Let's go swing on the big swings. You take him. I don't have a lap any more."

They sat on the big swings, side by side. William settled into Billy's arms.

"I saw Francis Clemens yesterday," she said.

"Really?" Penny said. "And what did he have to say for himself?"

"He said his children loved their snowsuits."

Penny arched her eyebrow.

"I saw him at that party," Billy said. "He took us out for a drink."

They swung for a while and watched the children climbing on the jungle gym. In their bright clothes, they looked like a flock of parrots.

"How was it?" Penny said.

"Seeing Francis?" said Billy. "He was with a really beautiful girl who turned out to be his daughter-in-law. I was extremely jealous."

"Hmm," said Penny. "What's that about?"

"When I think about him it's always in the past tense, but when I saw him I realized how *alive* these things are, even when they've ceased to be," Billy said. "The water doesn't close over your head. I mean, it doesn't close over mine. I realize that no matter what happens Francis is indelible. He's part of my experience—like seeing Stonehenge or traveling in India."

"Or going to college," said Penny.

"He was more like graduate school," Billy said.

She looked down and saw that she had swung William right to sleep. She felt her heart open and expand: she loved everyone—William, Grey, Penny, Francis. Her baby breathed against her. He was growing so fast he seemed to melt away before she could get used to him.

She wondered what William would look like at thirteen. She remembered Grey so clearly at that age with his wavy hair, and his round, wire-rimmed glasses and the ink stains on his fingers.

She looked over to the street and gave a start. She thought she saw Francis walking toward the park but it was only a man about Francis's height, wearing a familiar-looking coat.

A Note on the Type

The text of this book was set on the Linotype in Garamond No. 3, a modern rendering of the type first cut by Claude Garamond (ca. 1480–1561). Garamond was a pupil of Geoffroy Tory and is believed to have based his letters on the Venetian models, although he introduced a number of important differences. It is to him that we owe the letter known as "old style." He gave to his letters a certain elegance and feeling of movement that won for their creator an immediate reputation and the patronage of Francis I of France.

Composed by Maryland Linotype Composition Company, Baltimore, Maryland

Printed and bound by The Haddon Craftsmen, Inc., Scranton, Pennsylvania

Designed by Cecily Dunham